The Gingerbread Farm on the cover was
constructed by the author at Christmas, 2011.
The recipe and houseplans are on pages 37-40.
View the making of the Gingerbread Farm:
www.luckyvalleypress.com/gbf

Other books by Ginna BB Gordon

The Lavandula Series (print and ebook)
Novels based on the fictional journals of Stefani Michel
Book One: Looking for John Steinbeck
Book Two: Deke Interrupted
Book Three: Humming in Spanish (Fall 2020)

Bonnebrook
Book One in the
Honey Baby Darlin' Series
Lucky Valley Press

The Soup Kit
A portal to great soups
Lucky Valley Press

A Simple Celebration
the nutritional program for
the Chopra Center for Well Being
a vegetarian cookbook for
body, mind and spirit
Ginna Bell Bragg & David Simon, MD
Harmony Books/Random House

The Gingerbread Farm

**Farm Two in the
Honey Baby Darlin' Series**

A serial memoir about cooking,

love and the love of cooking

Ginna BB Gordon

The Gingerbread Farm

Copyright © 2012-2019 by Ginna BB Gordon

All rights reserved

Cover by David Gordon & Ginna BB Gordon

All photos and renderings are from
the collection of the author

ISBN#978-0-9856655-0-0

Lucky Valley Press
PO Box 671
Jacksonville, Oregon 97530
www.luckyvalleypress.com

Printed in U.S.A on acid-free paper.

Dedication

To my real-life
but long-departed parents,
Dick and Virginia,
and others
on whom the Gingerbread Farm
characters are based:
Thank you for allowing me to
evoke your essences and
beautiful memories
in print

to my son, Michael,
To Rosie,
and three girls,
Taylor, Devon and Sienna

and for Tim,
your star burns bright
1985-2011

GBBG

Author's Note

Honey Baby Darlin' is a four-part series about cooking, love and the love of cooking: a memoir, in which many beloved characters help develop a young girl's consciousness about food, the art of nurturing and the kitchen. It is not exactly autobiographical, but rather... evocative – Glory's back-stories give it time, place and feeling. The love is expansive, universal.

Glory (the alter-character, the me-not-me, Ginna-not-Ginna of this memoir) doesn't rummage around too deeply into the jumbled closet of her intimate relationships or existential questions, because, whatever she finds in that enormous pile is just one more shiny object, beckoning. Staying on topic (cooking, love and the love of cooking) is challenging. Like placing her shoes outside before entering the temple, Glory leaves her dramas and issues at the kitchen door. Well, most of them. She *is* human. If the shiny object (the remembered event or story) relates to a recipe or fabulous foodie thing, or leads her on her cooking, love and the love of cooking quest, it stays. Otherwise, it's saved as deep drama material for the novels awaiting their turn on the author's docket.

Ernest Hemingway's advice: "All you have to do is write one true sentence. Write the truest sentence you know." Glory's memoir evokes the truest part of my own cooking history – the characters, the challenges, the changes experienced in various kitchens over 60 years of eventful cooking.

Ginna BB Gordon

Introduction

The Gingerbread Farm, # 2 in the Honey Baby Darlin' series, picks up Glory's story a few years after the last lines of **Honey Baby Darlin' Book One - The Farm** come to a close... Little Glory is growing up, longing for her *life-to-be* – she loves the Farm, but strains against its confines.

In Honey Baby Darlin' Book One – The Farm, life was limned by Glory's parents, James and Gloria, whose prose and poetry brought them close during their Korean War separation: cooking kept Gloria busy; little Glory observed her mother and family, cooks and companions, from a four-year-old's perch at the kitchen counter in the Big House at the Farm.

The Gingerbread Farm, Farm finds Glory's sweaters too tight and her longing large. She's 12 going on 21, a young girl in a woman's body, with a love of books, interesting food and art.

Glory's diaries, letters and California journals allow tastes of her world (good tastes – hot cocoa with marshmallows kind of tastes) and the many boxes of cooking memorabilia inform the author. Glory Sugar Baker takes you back once again to her cooking history, to the people who have colored her kitchens, taught her the arts of nurturing, and the places and times in which they lived and played and cooked together.

Honey Baby Darlin' Book One covers an intense one-year period in the early fifties. **The Gingerbread Farm** explores the 60s and 70s: 20 years of cooking adventures - from Glory's grandfather's farm in Ohio to the Gingerbread Farm on California's beautiful Carmel Coastline.

This book includes **160+** recipes and a few historical nuggets, both culinary and pop-cultural.

"One cannot think well,

Love well,

Sleep well,

If one has not dined well."

Virginia Woolf

♥

"Love is not something

You think about-

It is a state

In which you dwell."

Joshua
Lamb
By Christopher Moore

Part One
1959-1965

June, 1959

My own,

I always have the feeling that something extraordinary should happen on our anniversaries, some planetary event. I watch for bursting rockets or shooting stars, winged angels flying out of fluffy white cakes, because I am sure the heavens are as glad as I am that we are married. But tomorrow, nothing unusual like that will happen. And it is just as well.

What will happen is much more desirable. You will smile at me. I'll wake up in the morning and you will be beside me, and you would do that for no one but me in this world. Glory or Martin will knock on the door for homework help, new ribbons, shoe polish, and any minute, the car keys. JR will wiggle his way under our covers for a snuggle – and soon enough, the car keys. The fact that such things happen every day is what makes life so sublime.

You are so fine, so decent, so pleasant (mornings before coffee the exception), so loving and lovable. I respect you – for your intelligence, your ideals, your principles, your integrity.

You are all that matters, and I have the privilege of making you happy.

Your fortunate husband

Angels from Heaven Cake

1 cup cake flour
3/4 cup sugar + 2 Tablespoons sugar
12 large egg whites
1 1/2 teaspoons cream of tartar
1/4 teaspoon salt
3/4 cup sugar
1 1/2 teaspoons vanilla

Angel Food cake pan
Heat oven to 375°

Sift cake flour and 3/4 cup + 2 Tablespoons sugar; set aside. Beat egg whites (be sure to keep all yolks out of the egg whites!), cream of tartar and salt until soft peaks are formed.

Slowly add the other 3/4 cup of sugar while beating on high until stiff peaks form. Beating on low, add flour mixture and vanilla slowly, folding in the sides and bottom of the batter as it forms.

Carefully spoon the batter into sprayed Angel Food cake pan.
Slide a knife through the batter to remove air pockets.
Bake 30-35 minutes or until the top springs back when touched lightly with your finger. Cool ten minutes.

Remove the cake from the pan by first running a knife around the edge. Whack the sides of the pan to loosen. Invert onto plate and gently tap.

1959

September 29
Bedtime
Dear Diary,

Today is my 12th birthday. This is page 1 of my new Diary - purple!

It has a lock. I should have some secrets!

Gloria says diaries are for writing deep thoughts and important events of the day. Poems and stuff. My family is big on poems.

Important Things List:

Fashion Tip of the Day
The Best of the Best Recipes
Who's cool
Who's not
Deep thoughts

Problem is, I have no deep thoughts and nothing ever happens here.

I'll write down my birthday dinner menu- that's deep.

For the 6th year in a row, my request:

Fried Chicken, Mashed Potatoes, Peas, Gravy, Boston Cream Pie.

And more really cool presents-
-From James –
        -a portable record player for my room!
I think he was making up for the other night when he was ~~enibriated~~,
~~inebri~~ – had tee many martoonies and got mad at me for no good reason.

-From Martin – sent from Kitchner Prep-
        -My 3rd annual plastic egg of Silly Putty,
        a set of colored pencils and a goofy card
        with a poem attached:

        I have a little sister
        She's growing up quite fast
        Once she was a little girl
        Now that is the past

        She is almost a teenager
        What will Mother do?
        And what will Father say to her?
        When she dyes her hair
                peacock blue

        I love my little sister
        And now a pretty girl
        But if she goes into my room
        I will feed her to the squirrels

        Ha Ha.
        Love,
        Martin

-Marnie –
     -- three blue lace-edged hankies, embroidered with GSB. Perfect.

-But the best –
     --Flossie, Bessie and Lincoln made me a quilt! I wondered what they were doing, Backstairs. I can see their bedroom lights from my room in the cottage, and they were still on at midnight a couple of nights in a row, when I got up to pee. Gloria would prefer I say "use the loo" or even better, "visit the powder room," but I am definitely not powdering anything in the middle of the night.

The quilt is patchwork, made out of my old dresses and shorts and shirts, which Lincoln saved for 8 years. He cut everything into six-inch squares and stacked them in his closet, waiting until there were enough pieces for Glory's History Quilt!

Ta Da! 8 years of my little life.

There are the checked shorts I wore to the 5th grade picnic last June when Dan Partrick kissed me on the cheek while we sat on a hay bale in the shade. My left cheek still burns at the thought. And here is my pink Dotted Swiss Easter dress, 1956, I think. And, Oh! The soft blue shirt I ruined at Girl Scout Camp – it has a little pucker in it.

My favorite cousin, Tournier, Junior, couldn't come for dinner tonight. It's a school night and besides, she's home sick with a cold. I would make her favorite Creamy Chicken Soup and Florida Orange Juice, guaranteed to make her well. But she's not here.

Creamy Chicken Soup

1/2 cup unsalted butter
1 medium yellow onion, chopped
2 stalks celery (including leaves), chopped
3 medium carrots, chopped
1/2 cup flour
6 cups chicken stock*
one small bundle of parsley, thyme, sage,
bay leaf and tarragon, tied with kitchen twine
3 cups cooked chicken, pulled from the bird
(rather than chopped)
1/2 cup heavy cream
2 1/2 teaspoons dry sherry
1 Tablespoon salt
freshly ground black pepper to taste
Italian parsley for garnish

In a large soup pot over medium heat, melt the butter to the smoking point – I love cooking with brown butter! Add the onion, celery, and carrots and cook, covered, stirring occasionally, until soft, about 15 minutes. Add the flour and stirring constantly, cook until bubbling and smooth – about 1 minute. Add stock slowly, stirring constantly and bring to a simmer. Tie the parsley sprigs, thyme, sage, bay leaf and tarragon together with a piece of kitchen twine and add to the soup. Lower the heat and simmer for 15 minutes.

Stir in the chicken and simmer. Stir in the heavy cream, sherry, and salt and pepper into the soup. Toss out the bundle of herbs. Serve immediately with chopped parsley. This soup can be blended before the chicken is added. Gloria says the sherry is essential for the final flavor blend.

** Honey Baby Darlin, Book One - The Farm, page 114*

Oh! And here's the blue chenille robe from that trip with Junior to Pop and Marnie's at the City House in like 1952, ancient history! They put a piece of Junior's pink robe in there, too. Kewt!

I think Junior's still ticked off at Gloria for making her at least try the Three Bean Salad last time she stayed here overnight, when Aunt T went to New York. Junior said it smelled like gasoline – not NY, but the Three Bean Salad. NY, too, I guess! Ha Ha!

Gloria stood by the table with what James calls her "Glorious Frown." Junior gagged.

I liked it, or at least I ate it, maybe so I could have the Baked Custard with Chocolate Chips, without the – uhm, what did Gloria call it? Wait while I look it up…

Histrionics! Yep. Junior was being t.h.e.a.t.r.i.c.a.l. She got the Custard anyway. All that drama for nothing.

Fashion Tip of the Day – put away your white shoes after Labor Day and don't wear them again 'til Easter.

Fashion Tip # 2 – well, not really a fashion tip, but a grandmother tip – A well put-together lady is never without a hankie. You never know when tears might spill. (Lace edged hankies are definitely not for honking and blowing!)

Three Bean Salad

1 15-ounce can cannellini
or white beans,
rinsed and drained
1 15-ounce can kidney
or black beans,
rinsed and drained
1 15-ounce can garbanzo beans,
rinsed and drained
2 celery stalks, chopped fine
1/2 sweet red onion, chopped fine
1 grated carrot
1 cup fresh,
finely chopped Italian parsley
1/3 cup apple cider vinegar
1/3 cup sugar
1/4 cup olive oil
1 1/2 teaspoons salt
1/4 teaspoon black pepper

Mix the beans, celery, onion, carrot and parsley in a large bowl. Whisk together the vinegar, sugar, olive oil, salt, and pepper in a separate small bowl. Add the dressing to the beans and gently toss to coat.

Chill in the refrigerator for several hours for absorption of flavors.

Baked Custard with Chocolate Chips

5 egg yolks
2 whole eggs
1 cup sugar
1 teaspoon vanilla
3 cups scalded milk
1/2 cup semi-sweet chocolate chips

Beat eggs, sugar and vanilla. Pour in milk. Pour into casserole or individual custard cups. Sprinkle with nutmeg. Place casserole or custard cups in a big shallow pan of hot water. Bake at 300° for 35-60 minutes. Done when knife comes out clean. Serve warm, sprinkled with chocolate chips. The chips melt into the custard, and you can swirl it around to make patterns.

The Gotham Hotel
Fifth Ave
New York
October 3rd, 1959

Dear SugarPop,

    Thanks for the box of stationery from the Gotham Hotel in New York. As you can see, I am putting it to good use. The fountain pen is cool, but I can't use it just now because my left-handed, cursive writing smears it all over the page. Please forgive the ballpoint pen, but it's less messy. The nuns have a humongous fit about my handwriting. Did you know the Romans considered anything on the left – like weapons (or pens even) to be unlucky? They said being left-handed is sinister! Oh brother. No wonder the nuns freak out about me.

    And thank you, too, for the real, authentic New York Cheesecake recipe. I just knew I was right about separating the eggs and whipping the egg whites, but Gloria didn't believe me! The other way is just a Midwestern Church Bazaar version or something, but not the real thing. This is the tall, fluffy version, in a spring-form pan, which is RIGHT, not a pie plate! You are the coolest grandfather on the very Earth!

Love, Glory B

Authentic New York Cheesecake

2 1/2 cups
crushed graham crackers
1 stick melted butter
2 Tablespoons sugar
24 ounces cream cheese
1 cup sugar
4 egg yolks
1/4 cup heavy cream
4 egg whites
1/4 - 1/2 teaspoon
cream of tartar
1 teaspoon vanilla

1 cup sour cream
1 teaspoon vanilla
2 Tablespoons sugar

In a bowl, blend together crushed graham crackers, melted butter and sugar.

Beat cream cheese and sugar. Blend in egg yolks and heavy cream. Whip the 4 egg whites and cream of tartar. Add vanilla. Gently fold half into cream cheese mixture, then the other half.

Press graham cracker crust into bottom of large spring-form pan, pressing up sides 1/2 inch. Gently pour cream cheese mixture into crust. Bake at 350° for 1 hour 15 minutes or until golden brown and cracked on top.

Mix sour cream, vanilla and sugar and spread on top. Put back in oven at 425° for 5 minutes. Chill before serving. Or not. 12 pieces.

October 11th, 1959
Dear Diary,

Junior is spending the night. She gave me a red and white striped
Hula Hoop for my birthday! She brought one for herself, too, in yellow
stripes, and we spent the entire day hula-hula-hula-hooping around
the Cypress trees in the front yard of the Big House, trying not to fall
down laughing! Major, usually a dignified pooch, actually barked at
me! We were beyond crazy!

The King and I "original motion picture soundtrack" LP came in the
mail today - a surprise from Gloria and James to go with my record
player. This is a humongously wonderful thing! I am playing it right
this minute! Junior's lying on my new quilt of personal historical
reference with her eyes closed, dreaming of Yul Brynner's beautiful,
shiny bald head, I am sure. I have been Deborah Kerr and Rita
Moreno, depending, for about two hours, leaping around my room with
various towels and scarves draped over my head for dramatic emphasis.
I can listen over and over, and sing even, and no one cares! I love it!
I don't know why. It's music that makes me cry and laugh and want
to hug people and learn the words and sing and dance and play the
piano, which is too bad, because I am all thumbs at the piano and gave
it up three years ago, and my voice cracks like a boy in puberty and
dance is now out of the question, with these boobs. Maybe I'll be a great
dramatic actress.

Dinner's ready! We've got to skedaddle up to the Big House for Marnie's favorite Saturday Night Dinner – Waffles, Scrambled Eggs, Bacon, and Fruit Salad. Last Saturday Night we had Ebelskivers filled with meat and cheese. Sometimes she likes James' World Famous Pancakes,* maybe Flossie's Orange Overnight French Toast, but Marnie's favorite Saturday Night always has something to do with Maple Syrup and Bacon!

Quick Fashion Tip: Don't wear high heels on a date with a short boy. (As if it mattered. I've never been on a date. Or worn heels.)

Junior and family are moving to Cleveland to be closer to the Sugar Empire. Botheration.

GB

*Honey Baby Darlin' Book One – The Farm, page 279

Waffles

1 3/4 cups all-purpose flour
1 3/4 teaspoons baking powder
1/8 teaspoon fine salt
1/8 teaspoon ground nutmeg
1 1/2 cups milk,
at room temperature
2 large eggs,
at room temperature,
separated
1/2 teaspoon vanilla
1/4 cup unsalted butter, melted,
plus more for brushing the waffle iron
1/4 cup sugar

Preheat waffle iron.

In a large bowl, whisk together flour, baking powder, salt, and nutmeg.

In a medium bowl, whisk together milk, egg yolks, vanilla, and 1/4 cup melted butter. Whisk the milk mixture into the flour mixture to make a batter. Don't overbeat.

With an eggbeater or whisk, whip egg whites until they hold a loose peak. Sprinkle the sugar over the whites and continue beating until they hold a soft peak. With a spatula, fold 1/3 of the egg whites into the batter. Fold in the remaining whites.

Brush the hot surface of the iron with butter. Pour in about 1/3 to 3/4 cup batter to cover the surface of the iron. (The batter will spread when the lid is closed.) Cover and cook about 5 minutes, until golden brown. Repeat with the remaining batter. Serve immediately with breakfast condiments: syrup, jam, butter, fresh fruit, yogurt or sour cream.

Ebelskivers

1 3/4 cups all-purpose flour
3/4 teaspoon baking soda
1 teaspoon baking powder
1 1/2 Tablespoons granulated sugar
1/2 teaspoon salt
3 eggs, separated
1 3/4 cups buttermilk
4 Tablespoons (1/2 stick)
unsalted butter, melted
1 pint fresh blueberries
powdered sugar
and maple syrup

Whisk together the flour, baking soda, baking powder, granulated sugar and salt in a medium bowl.

Whisk together the egg yolks and buttermilk. Whisk the yolk mixture into the flour mixture until well combined; the batter will be lumpy.

In another bowl, beat the egg whites with your mixer on high speed until stiff peaks form, 2 to 3 minutes. Using a rubber spatula, gently fold the whites into the batter in two parts.

With baking spray or butter, grease each well of an Ebelskivers pan. Heat the pan and pour 1 tablespoon of batter into each well. Cook 3 to 5 minutes, until golden. Put filling (fruit, meat, cheese, veggies – in this case, blueberries) in the center of each pancake and top with 1 Tbs. batter. Turn over with a chopstick or knitting needle and cook until golden and crispy, about 3 minutes more. Transfer to a plate. Repeat with the remaining batter and filling.

Dust the pancakes with confectioners' sugar and serve warm with maple syrup. Makes about 40 little Ebelskivers.

Orange Overnight French Toast

1/4 cup (1/2 stick) butter,
room temperature
12 3/4-inch-thick
French bread slices, dried
6 eggs
1 1/2 cups milk
1/4 cup maple syrup
1 teaspoon orange zest
1/2 teaspoon salt
powdered sugar

Arrange bread slices in baking sheet or half-size "hotel pan." Beat eggs, milk, syrup, orange zest and salt in large bowl. Pour mixture over bread. Turn bread slices to coat. Cover with plastic and refrigerate overnight.

Preheat oven to 400°. Transfer soaked bread slices to another, butter-coated or sprayed pan. Bake 10 minutes. Carefully turn bread over and continue baking until just golden, about 5 minutes longer. Transfer cooked toast to plates and sprinkle with Powdered Sugar. Serve warm with Maple Syrup and butter and....strawberries and...

Tips on Making Bacon

Cover a sheet pan with baking parchment. Lay out the bacon very close together, but not overlapping. Bake at 325° for about 20 minutes. Remove from pan when done to the favored crispness and drain on paper towels. This is less greasy, easier to do, cleans up well and the bacon is flat!

Serve with something and maple syrup!

October 12th, 1959
Dear Diary,

I want to **be** Anna Leonowens, honored schoolteacher of King Mongkut's 55 or whatever Siamese children.

Let me think why. Is that important enough to write in a diary? A deep thought? She's beautiful and reads and wears glasses and she knows a lot of cool things. She's brave. She's sure of herself. She can whistle.

Shoot! She's 150 years old!

Halloween 1959
Dear Diary,

This is my first Halloween without Martin. I'm not dressing up – too much trouble. I've been sick with a code in da node and don't much care. It's Gloria's turn in the Hood to host a little pahtee, so maybe I'll go downstairs and sit by the fire under my quilt. Or, maybe not. I have my box of pencils and some new paper doll clothing designs to color in. Betsy McCall.

Gloria's Apple Fritters smell good, though. And she made me Chicken Soup. Hmmm... let me see. Marnie's bed or the fireplace... Marnie's bed or the fireplace...

Apple Fritters

2 cups sifted all-purpose flour
1/2 cup sugar
2 teaspoons salt
3 teaspoons baking powder
2/3 cup milk
2 eggs
2 cups finely chopped apple
1 cup confectioners' sugar, sifted

Sift together the flour, sugar, salt, and baking powder. Add milk and egg; beat until batter is smooth. Fold in chopped apple. Drop by teaspoonful into hot oil about 3 inches deep and fry for 2 to 3 minutes, until golden brown. Drain well on paper towels and roll in confectioners' or cinnamon sugar while still warm. Serve plain or with syrup.

Later....
Francene and Carmen came over for Gloria's party and perked me up a little. They looked so kewt! in their kitty outfits - Francene's face was painted white with a little black nose and gray whiskers and she had this long, grey knitted tail that dragged on the floor. Carmen's tail stuck up in the air like a bobcat. She didn't want to sit down, 'cause the wire stuck her in the rear, she said.

Carmen's mother brought over a Peach Crumble that was so good I wanted to take a bath in it. Then I found out it was Gloria's Peach Schnapps Crumble recipe! Ha Ha!

Peach Schnapps Crumble

4 cups peeled,
sliced fresh peaches
1 cup sugar
1/4 cup flour
pinch salt
sprinkle of cinnamon
2 Tablespoons Peach Schnapps
1/4 cup butter, cut in pieces

Combine the peaches, sugar, flour, salt, cinnamon and Peach Schnapps and in a bowl and mix well. Pour into buttered baking dish, dot with butter. Sprinkle liberally with Crumble Topping.

Bake at 350° for about 25 minutes, until golden and bubbly. Serve warm.

Crumble Topping

2 cups flour
1 cup cold, unsalted butter
1 cup sugar
1 teaspoon cinnamon

Blend all ingredients in food processor until crumbly, less than a minute. (Do not over blend - will become too doughy.)

❛

Thanksgiving, 1959
Dear Diary,

I am reading Catcher in the Rye. Gloria says it is too mature for me, but I like reading about someone's Existential ANGST. I like the word. ANGST. So many consonants. Well, it's German, anyway. I looked it up. It means Oh my God. Why am I here? What am I doing? What's the point? I think. Anyway, Holden Caulfield is a mixed-up, unhappy person, who hasn't figured out the point.

I haven't either, but that's OK.

Martin is home for the weekend with two friends from Kitchner, and he looks all grown up. 14. I think he shaves! He parades around in his uniform like he was a real Army major and holds the door open for Gloria. He cracks me up! He got Daddy to promise a BBQ on Saturday night, to make him burgers.

Imagine. A BBQ in November.

There's snow on the ground!

But, I guess he really missed James' burgers for breakfast.

James' Famous Burgers

Four pounds fresh ground chuck
1/3 cup each
carrots, onions & celery,
chopped fine and
sautéed in
two tablespoons olive oil
Cool and toss with
ground meat and
salt and pepper.
Form patties.

Tips on Burgers

Use fresh ground chuck with a high fat content for juiciness.
Before forming patties, chill the beef. Wash your hands well, form the
patties, then wash your hands again. Or use gloves. (It's a good idea to
have a box of surgical or kitchen gloves in the drawer with your foil).

Make each patty by forming about 1/4 pound of ground chuck into a
tight ball about the size of a tennis ball. Press it flat between layers of
parchment paper.

Use a spoon to flatten the sides of the patty.

Form patties larger than your buns to allow for shrinkage. Season the
burgers on both sides with salt and pepper. Kosher salt and freshly
ground black pepper give the best flavor.

Spray the bars of the grill with canola or other baking spray. Then build a
hot fire.

Cook burger about 3 to 4 minutes per side, turning once. Don't press
down or squeeze out the juices while cooking your burgers. Excellent for
breakfast, lunch or dinner!

Buns for Burgers or Hot Dogs

2 tablespoons sugar
2 packets active dry yeast
1/2 cup lukewarm water
2 cups lukewarm milk
2 tablespoons vegetable oil
2 teaspoons salt
6 to 7 1/2 cups flour

Egg wash: 1 egg beaten with 1 Tablespoon cold water
sesame, poppy or caraway seeds or coarse salt (optional)

Dough should be quite soft and relaxed to make soft and tender buns. Add only enough flour beyond 6 cups to make the dough knead-able.

In a large bowl, dissolve the sugar and yeast in the warm water. Add the milk, oil, and 3 cups of flour to the yeast mixture. Beat vigorously for 2 minutes.

Add the salt and gradually add flour, 1/4 cup at a time, until the dough begins to pull away from the sides of the bowl. Turn the dough out onto a floured board.

Knead until dough is smooth and elastic.

Put the dough into an oiled bowl, turning once to coat the entire ball of dough with oil. Cover with a damp towel and let rise until doubled, about one hour.

Turn the dough out onto a lightly floured work surface. Divide into 18 equal pieces.

Shape each piece into a ball. For hamburger buns, flatten the balls into three-inch disks. For hot-dog buns, roll the balls into cylinders, 4 1/2 inches in length. Flatten the cylinders slightly; dough rises more in the center so this will give a gently rounded top versus a high top.

For soft-sided buns, place them on a well-seasoned baking sheet a half an inch apart so they'll grow together when they rise. For crisper buns, place them three inches apart.

Second Rising: Cover with a towel and let rise until almost doubled, about 45 minutes.

Preheat oven to 400°. Just before baking, lightly brush the tops of the buns with the egg wash and sprinkle with seeds, if desired.

Bake for 20 minutes. When the buns are done, remove them from the baking sheet to cool on a wire rack, to prevent the crust from becoming soggy.

Sunday, after Thanksgiving
Dear Diary,

This is so entirely funny. James made pancakes on Thanksgiving morning. We all sat around the counter at the Big House – Me, Martin, his friends, Tom and Josh, and JR. As usual, there were big bowls of strawberries, sour cream, bacon and sausages, and a bazillion platters of the World's Greatest Pancakes,* which Daddy thinks of as his own personal nobel-prize winning contribution to the world. Anyway, he stands at the counter in his wrap-around apron, presiding like a chef boss over his precious pancake griddle, making dollar-sized cakes until the batter is all gone, scraped down to the last little drop in the bowl. He says pancakes left on the platter are an insult to the pancake-maker - that's him. And there we were, passing the last five little cakes back and forth across the counter. But, we were all stuffed! We were whispering to each other...

You eat them!

No, you!

I can't!

Please, he'll have hurt feelings!

Can't. Try JR!

No. So, I got creative through desperation. When James wasn't looking, I opened the drawer under the counter and tossed the cakes in. Later on, I came back to the kitchen, put the soggy pancakes in my pocket and threw them out into the snow behind the cottage. The birds will love them, I thought to myself. And Daddy won't be insulted.

***Honey Baby Darlin' Book One – The Farm page 279**

This morning, at the breakfast table, Daddy smiled and cleared
his throat to get the attention of his audience. We thought some big
announcement was about to be made – like John Beresford Tipton had
just sent Michael Anthony to deliver a check for a million dollars, or
he was buying Martin a green MG, the car of his dreams. We were all
expectant. Something cool was about to happen.

He looked around the table at each one of us – Martin, Tom, Josh, me,
even JR - and then said, "I... beg to know... with a bereaved heart, why
there are five pancakes on the ground outside my bedroom window."

Melting snow is not my friend.

The night before
the night before Christmas, 1959
Dear Diary,

Tonight I have to babysit JR. I like him
and all, but it's so not cool that Gloria
doesn't pay me, since I have become a
professional babysitter now. I make $2 an
hour babysitting those cute little Oakes
girls next door, so Gloria owes me like,
$4,000 for all the times I've taken care of
the little burger.

Two days from now is Christmas and the Big House kitchen is, as usual,
full of flour and sugar and chocolate. Gloria is making her 20th annual
Gloria's Gloria. The dining room is full of baskets and liners and jars of
this and that (jams and jelly and Lemon Curd, yum, my favorite). She
added some new cookies this year. It's fun to watch JR eat cookies.

And, oh, this is the BEST! The day after Christmas, Junior and Little
Jon are coming to make Gingerbread Houses and Ornaments! Gloria
says if we make ornaments now, we can paint them all year to be ready
for Christmas 1960!! I am sooo excited. And, she says the Gingerbread
Houses are fantasies and ~~efem~~ ephemeral, which means they won't last,
and aren't for eating, really. I don't care about eating it. I just want to
build it! Besides, the funny thing is, there is no ginger in the gingerbread
recipe! Ha Ha. We made the dough today so it can "rest." It's like mixing
concrete for slabs!

Holiday Ornaments a la Gloria Sugar Baker

1 cup salt
2 cups flour
1 cup water
2 Tablespoons
vegetable oil
water-based paints

Place dry ingredients in a bowl, add the water and oil, stir until blended. Once the dough holds together, Roll into a ball and kneed it to make a smooth texture.

Place the dough on a cutting-board, roll the dough out a bit thicker than for regular cookies. Cut out the ornaments with cookie cutters or design your own by shaping dough with your fingers.

Don't forget to punch or carve a hole into the top of the ornament for a string to go through to hang the beautiful decoration on your tree!

Bake at 250° until hard and dry but not browned - one or two hours. Cool completely and paint with water-based paints or glue on glitter using white household glue. Thread a string or ribbon through the hole and hang the decoration on the tree

Ornament ideas:

Stars, Hearts, Ducks, Twisted Candy Canes, Trees, Gingerbread Boys & Girls, Big Foot!

Rice Krispies Chocolate Bars

3 Tablespoons butter
1 bag marshmallows
6 cups Rice Krispies
1/2 cup chocolate chips

In large saucepan melt butter over low heat. Add marshmallows and stir until completely melted. Remove from heat.

Add Rice Krispies and chocolate chips. Stir until well coated.

Using buttered spatula press mixture into 13 x 9 x 2-inch pan coated with baking spray. Cool. Cut into 2-inch squares.

Lemon Curd

3 large lemons
1/2 cup butter
1 1/2 cups sugar
3 egg yolks, beaten

Wash the lemons and zest the rinds. Squeeze the lemons and strain the juice into the top of a double boiler. Add the zested peel, butter, sugar and egg yolks. Cook, stirring constantly, until the butter melts, the sugar dissolves and the curd begins to thicken, about five minutes. Don't let it boil – this will curdle the eggs. When the Lemon Curd is thick and creamy, immediately pour into a clean glass jar. Cover the curd with a towel or plastic wrap to keep a skin from forming, let cool, and then refrigerate. Curd will last in refrigerator about three weeks. This makes about three cups. Gloria made it by the bucketful!

Author's Note: Meyer Lemons make a delicious Curd. They have thinner, more orangey skins, a cross between a lemon and a tangerine.

Gingerbread Boys & Girls

4 cups flour
pinch of salt
2 teaspoons ground ginger
1 teaspoon ground allspice
2 teaspoons baking soda
1/2 cup butter
1/3 cup brown sugar
1/4 cup sugar
1/4 cup dark molasses
1 egg, beaten

Preheat oven to 350°. Prepare sheet pans with baking spray.

Sift dry ingredients into a large bowl. Cook butter, all the sugars and molasses together in a saucepan until butter melts. Pour mixture into bowl, add the beaten egg and blend well. Knead lightly to form dough. Roll out dough to 1/8 inch thickness. Cut with Gingerbread boy & girl cookie cutters, or pumpkin cookie cutters, or whatever! Bake about 12 minutes – don't burn the bottoms! Use glacé icing (sifted powdered sugar and a little water to make a thick icing) for buttons and face. Apply with a pastry tube or plastic container with applicator point.

Gingerbread House

(Enlarge plans to suit needs)
Structure (walls, roof, chimney, trees, etc.)

18 cups flour
18 Tablespoons double-acting baking powder
6 teaspoons ground cinnamon
6 teaspoons ground cloves
1 1/2 teaspoons ground nutmeg
1 1/2 teaspoons ground cardamom
1 teaspoon salt
1 3/4 cups dark molasses
4 3/4 cups sugar (may be half brown sugar)
3/4 cup butter
1 cup fresh lemon juice
3 Tablespoons grated lemon peel
3 eggs
3 egg yolks

This recipe makes enough for three small houses.

Cut out Gingerbread House templates in cardboard and make sure they fit together.

Gingerbread House-Plans 1

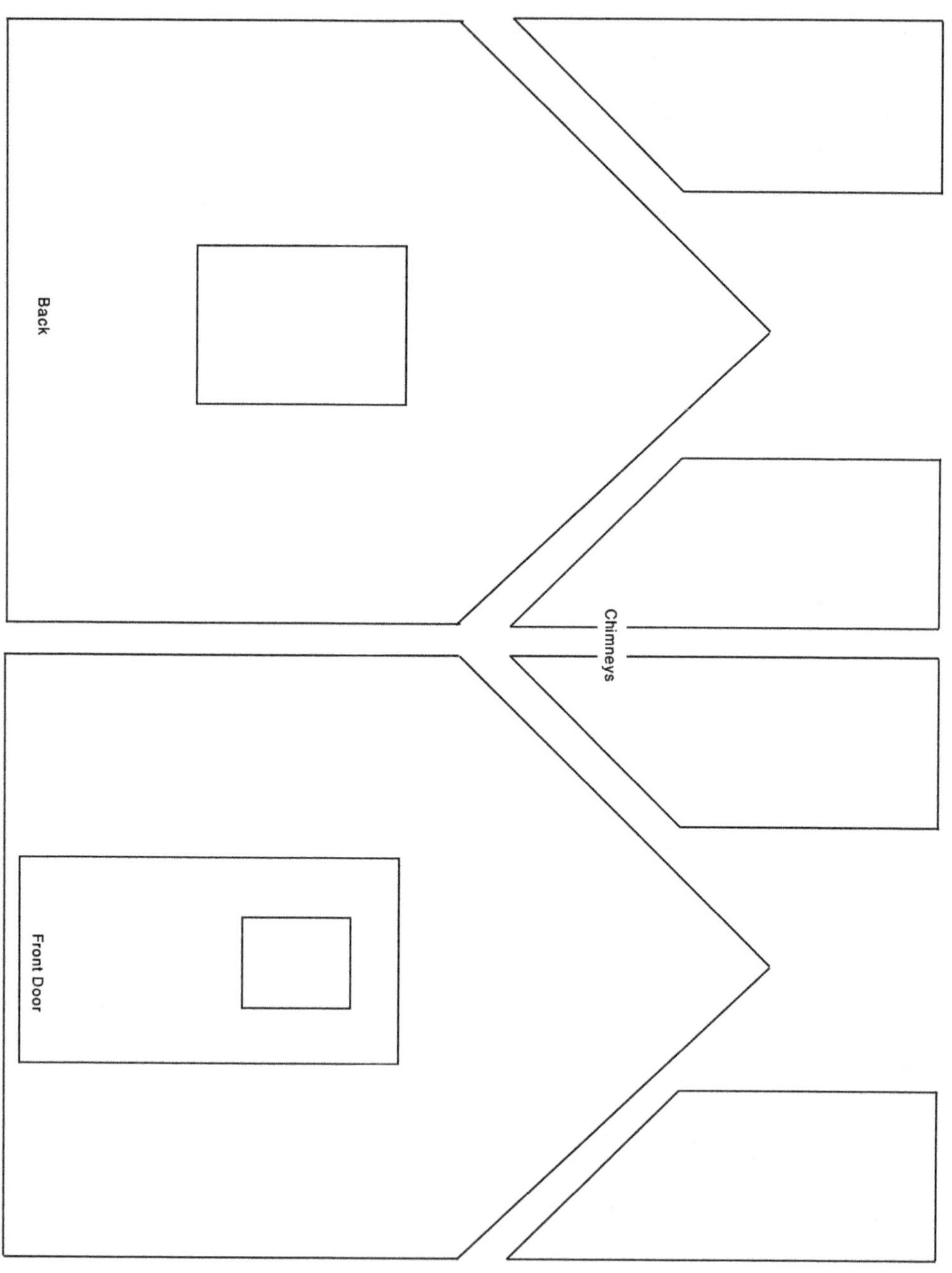

Gingerbread House –Plans 2

Side Panels and supports

Cut gingerbread men, Christmas Trees, elves, etc. here

These plans are not to scale and are meant as a general guideline for the parts you will need.

Gingerbread House-Plans 3

Decorations:

gum drops
cinnamon sticks
almonds, blanched or slivered
walnuts
stick cookies
M&Ms
green sprinkles
chocolate stick cookies
Marzipan or Fondant edible clay
for little animals and windowsills
pretzels
Red Hots
...and any other sweet thing
that strikes your fancy
and looks like it belongs
on a Gingerbread House.

PS: Since there is no ginger in the gingerbread recipe, and it is designed to last for years, I do not recommend eating it. It tastes like sawdust, which is good, I guess, for a house.

Preheat oven to 350°. Line three sheet pans with parchment.

Sift flour, spices, baking powder and salt into a large mixing bowl. Place molasses, brown sugar and butter in saucepan to melt butter and blend. Cool. Add egg and lemon juice and pour into dry ingredients. Mix well to form a soft dough. This dough can rest overnight.

Knead on floured surface and divide into three equal pieces. On floured surface, roll out dough and press into sheet pans. They should be about 1/4 inch thick. Bake about twenty minutes, or until firm and golden. Let cool about five minutes.

Using the cardboard cut-outs, cut warm cake in the pan into shapes for the sides, roof, and supports of the house. Be sure to cut out any windows and doors while the cake is still warm.

Royal Icing:

8 egg whites
12 cups sifted powdered sugar
4 teaspoons lemon juice
4 teaspoons Glycerin
(keeps the icing white)

Beat egg whites in bowl. Slowly add in, while beating, powdered sugar, lemon juice and Glycerin. Makes a stiff icing. To prevent drying out, keep icing in plastic containers with lids. Working on a cake board, cutting board or piece of wood covered with parchment; use icing to glue house panels and pieces together:

Glue corner supports to insides of front and back panels, 1/4 inch in from the edge. Attach side panels, butting them up to the corner supports.

Spread icing liberally onto one panel at a time. Let set before you begin adding decorations, using sticks to support windows, etc.

With icing, attach roof panels. Glue chimney pieces together with icing and attach to roof.

Decorate at will, using cut outs to represent gingerbread men, trees, fences, logs, whatever you can think of.

This is enough Royal Icing to glue together three small Gingerbread Houses. The icing will last for several weeks in the refrigerator while you design your masterpiece.

1960

July 12, 1960
Dear Diary,

Martin and Gloria are making a mess. They are refinishing my bedroom furniture in a French provincial style – basically, they are making my new furniture look old by painting it white and then dirtying it up with brown stain. This is for some kind of surprise. I don't know what. I tried to help, but they didn't go for that. Martin gave me a dollar and told me to go write a book on How to Be Obnoxious. Am I a pain? It's MY furniture!

So, OK.

How to Be Obnoxious in 10 Easy Lessons.
My first official book, for which I was paid $1 in advance.
12 pages. Stapled.

1. Pester your brother until he pays you to go away.
2. Play with the dog near someone painting furniture.
3. Stare at your brother while he's trying to ignore you.
4. Eat chocolate cake in front of someone with paint on his hands.

more...

Sour Cream Chocolate Cake

1 cup baking cocoa
1 cup boiling water
1 cup butter, softened
2 1/2 cups sugar
4 eggs
2 teaspoons vanilla extract
3 cups cake flour
2 teaspoons baking soda
1/2 teaspoon baking powder
1/2 teaspoon salt
1 cup sour cream

Dissolve cocoa in water; let stand until cool. In a large mixing bowl, cream butter and sugar until light and fluffy. Add eggs, one at a time, beating well after each. Add vanilla. Combine the flour, baking soda, baking powder and salt; add to creamed mixture alternately with sour cream, beating well. Add cocoa mixture; beat well.

Pour into three greased and floured 9-in. round baking pans. Bake at 350° for 30-35 minutes or until a toothpick inserted near the center comes out clean. Cool for 10 minutes before removing from pans to wire racks to cool completely.

Frosting

2 cups semisweet chocolate chips
1/2 cup butter
1 cup sour cream
1 teaspoon vanilla extract
4 1/2 cups confectioners' sugar

In a heavy saucepan, melt chocolate chips and butter over low heat; stir until smooth. Remove from the heat; cool for 5 minutes. Place in a large mixing bowl; add sour cream and vanilla; beat until blended. Add confectioners' sugar; beat until light and fluffy. Spread between layers and over top and sides of cake.

July 30, 1960
Dear Diary,

We are building a house! Wowie Zow! My dirtied-up-on-purpose furniture will look so beaoootiful in my special new room! What a great surprise!!!!

5. Act and be smarter than your brothers!

Gloria is designing the house with Mr. McTaggert, who taught me how to do the Twist (Chubby Checker, C'mon Baby!) and how to make raviolis from scratch! He even gave me his rolling pin ravioli-maker thingy-ma-bob.

6. Spy on your brother when he is with his friends, especially if it is a girl.

7. Dance better than your brother – no problem there. Boogie-woogie.

SugarPop gave Gloria and James a three-acre lot facing the backside of the Big House. I am happy, 'cause I'll have this big, cool room on the second floor, with maple flooring, and I get to pick out the wallpaper and the other "elements." I am sad though, because this means the beginning of the end of the Farm. Pop is dividing it up into lots and selling them. He must be feeling old – he's at least 60, and is tired of the upkeep and the driving back and forth from the City House in Rocky River to the Farm in Bath. So, someday soon, someone else will live here and our new house will face the backside of THEIR FARM HOUSE. This very much rattles my cage. Tomorrow we are going shopping for wallpaper.

8. Know how to make ravioli since someone else you know doesn't.

9. Talk on the phone for hours on end so other people can't call their girlfriends.

10. In general, try to do everything better than uhm... other people.

GB

3 cups white flour
1 teaspoon salt
4 eggs
2 Tablespoons olive oil

1 yolk, for egg wash

Combine flour and salt in a bowl. Add eggs 1 at a time and mix into flour. Drizzle in oil and continue to incorporate into the flour until it forms a ball. Sprinkle flour on work surface; knead the dough until smooth and elastic. Wrap the dough in plastic and let it rest for about 30 minutes.

Cut the ball of dough in half, cover what you are not using. Dust surface and dough with flour. Form the dough into a rectangle and roll it out thin, thin, thin. The dough should be 1/8 to 1/4 inch thick. Mr. McTaggert did his by-hand; today I would use a pasta machine.

Dust the counter and dough with flour; lay out the long sheet of pasta. Brush the top surface of dough with egg wash. Place 1 tablespoon of cooled filling about 2 inches apart on half the sheet of pasta. Fold the unfilled half over the filling. Using a rolling pin ravioli maker, press the dough together around each bit of filling. Cut through the pressed dough to make ravioli squares. Make sure the crimped edges are well sealed before cooking so the filling doesn't leak out. If making in advance of serving, dust with cornmeal to prevent sticking.

Cook the ravioli in boiling salted water for 10 to 15 minutes. Ravioli will float to the top when cooked. Gently remove the ravioli from water with slotted spoon. Serve immediately.

Filling ideas:

4 Tablespoons butter
3 Tablespoons, shallots, finely chopped
1 cup roasted butternut squash puree
salt
pepper
1/4 cup heavy cream
3 Tablespoons grated Parmesan cheese
pinch nutmeg
1 recipe pasta dough,
rolled out into wide ribbons,
about 1/4 inch thick

12 fresh sage leaves
1 Tablespoon finely chopped
fresh parsley leaves

Melt 1 tablespoon of the butter in a heavy bottomed saucepan. Add the shallots and sauté for 1 minute. Add the squash puree and cook about 2 to 3 minutes. Stir in the cream and cook for 2 minutes. Remove from the heat and stir in 3 tablespoons cheese and nutmeg, to taste. Add herbs. Cool before filling pasta sheets.

Also:

finely chopped leftover meats sautéed with onions, etc.
three cheeses (Parmesan, Ricotta & Mozzarella)

September 29, 1960
Dear Diary,

I am 13. I am now an official teenager.

When Aunt T went to China this summer, she fell in love with Hot
& Sour Soup and for my birthday, brought me a recipe to add to
my "Cures From Nature" folder, since the Chinese put lots of ginger
in it and this is supposed to be good for you and is like our Chicken
Soup cure, which is credited to the Jewish people, but I have borrowed
it, because I know it works. Just ask Junior. Aunt T is so cool – she
actually believes me when I tell her I will be a chef someday. Uncle Jon
makes fun of me and calls me Chef and Chief and Big Chief Morning
Glory. So it's Chief and Junior. Tch. Oh well.

Hot & Sour Soup

1 block firm tofu
2 ounces cooked pork tenderloin

Marinade:
1 teaspoon soy sauce
1/2 teaspoon sesame oil
1 teaspoon or cornstarch

1/2 cup bamboo shoots
2 Tablespoons black fungus (Wood Ear)
or Cloud Ear fungus*
(or 3 - 4 Chinese dried black mushrooms
or fresh mushrooms)*
1 small handful
dried lily buds*
6 cups chicken stock
1 teaspoon salt, or to taste
1 teaspoon granulated sugar
2 Tablespoons soy sauce
2 Tablespoons rice vinegar
1 Tablespoon cornstarch
dissolved in 1/4 cup water
1 egg, beaten
1 green onion, finely chopped
white pepper to taste
hot chili oil, to taste, optional

Ingredients with a * are the hard-to-find things,
not in the Acme Market or Piggly Wiggly.

Shred pork. Mix marinade ingredients and marinate pork for 20 minutes.

Cut tofu into bite-sized cubes. Cut bamboo shoots into thin, fine slices. Soak fungus, in warm water for 20 minutes. Rinse, and cut into thin pieces. (If using Chinese dried mushrooms, soak, then cut off the stems and cut them into thin strips. If using fresh mushrooms, just brush and slice.)

Bring the stock to a simmer. Add bamboo shoots, fungus or mushrooms, and the lily buds, if you have them. (You can make a more Americanized version without these things, but Aunt T drove me all over Akron to find lily buds!) Stir. Add tofu. Simmer and add the marinated pork.

Stir in the salt, sugar, soy sauce and vinegar and sesame oil.

Mix the cornstarch with water. While stirring, slowly add the cornstarch mixture to the soup. Bring back to a simmer and remove from heat. Slowly drop in the beaten egg, stirring in one direction at the same time. Add the green onion and the white pepper to taste. Serve with chili oil. (Hot and Sour Soup can be frozen without the tofu. Add it when thawed and reheating for serving.)

March 15, 1962

Dearest Junior,

Well, I am excited!! I am in a play! I have a part in **High Ground**, this really cool mystery about a nun who finds the real killer. It all takes place in a convent where this prisoner and her guards are trapped by a flood. Sarat Carn is on her way to the gallows for the murder of her own brother. But a brilliant nun, Sister Mary Bonaventure, that's me, believes Sarat is innocent. She, like, uncovers this evidence and frees Sarat from certain death!

I get to spend the afternoons at the convent and study in a little guest room and have dinner with the nuns and then go to rehearsal in the evening! Last night I even had to spend the night because of a spring snow-storm (Ha! Just like in the play! I just thought of that!). Oh, and I get to wear a habit! Not truly an authentic one to the story, because my nuns are Dominican and the heroine is a Sister of Charity or Mercy or something, whose habits have these goofy wingy things instead of veils, but, heck... we have lots of Dominican habits, and no Sisters of Charity, so, I will be a Dominican.

Last night, I tried on the habit I will wear, and, since I asked for it all to be really authentic? They even gave me nuns' "undergarments"!!! This is truly amazing, because I did not know that nuns wear these dainty, hand-embroidered camisoles and slips and stuff – with little pink flowers and leaves and vines and whatever all along the edges, which they embroider themselves because they must be otherwise bored to tears when they are not praying or singing or teaching. I always thought (when I ever thought about it, which was probably not ever) that they wore muslin or coarse cotton, really plain and boring "undergarments." I brought home a garter belt with sort of thick white stockings (I told Sister Augustine they should try pantyhose, but she had never heard of them!) and a pink embroidered full slip and, of course, these ugly black brogans that make up for all the daintiness because one cannot do anything but galumph around in brogans, and a veil and scapula and everything.

I've had dinner in the nuns' refectory three nights a week for three
weeks - nun food. Paris Dressing (is there Paris Dressing in Paris?), it
comes out of a bottle, but it's good, and we have things like **Stuffed Bell
Peppers** and **Mac & Cheese** and **Red Flannel Hash** – cheap and filling
for a whole lot of nuns! 50 nuns at the Lady of Maples Convent, and not
one is skinny!

I hope you can come down from the Land of Cleve for the play. It'll be
in three weeks, and I'll ask Gloria to ask Aunt T to bring you, maybe
for the weekend, so you can help me get into my habit and see the play
three times!

Love, Chief

P.S. Is this typewriter cool, or what?
Now you'll get longer letters from me,
since I don't have to worry so much
about smearing ink or pencil lead down
the page! And it's red! And portable!
And I can keep copies of everything for
my memory "Box" which is already two
boxes. I wish you were here.

P.P.S. Sister William is so cool. She even had to teach one of the boys
borrowed for the play from St. Luke's Boys School how to swear with
meaning! Have you ever heard a nun swear? She is not inhibited. I
want to be like her when I grow up.

Only not a nun.

Stuffed Bell Peppers
3 servings, not enough for 50 nuns

3 large bell peppers,
red, yellow or green
1 cup boiling, salted water
2 Tablespoons canola
or vegetable oil
1/2 pound ground beef
1 carrot, chopped
1 small yellow onion, chopped
1 stalk celery, chopped
1 8 ounce can tomato sauce
2 cups breadcrumbs
2 Tablespoons melted butter

Heat oven to 350°

Cut a slice off the top of each pepper, remove pithy part and wash inside and out. Cook peppers in boiling water for five minutes and drain. Sauté beef and vegetables in hot oil. Mix in tomato sauce and 1/2 of the breadcrumbs. Salt to taste. Stuff peppers with filling. Mix remaining breadcrumbs with melted butter. Stand Peppers upright in oiled baking dish. Top with buttered breadcrumbs. Bake covered for 30 minutes; remove cover and bake an additional 15 minutes. Serve with Baked Potatoes and salad.

Mac & Cheese

2 cups cooked pasta, penne,
elbows or bows
1/4 cup butter
1/4 cup unbleached white flour
1/2 teaspoon salt
1/2 teaspoon mustard
1/4 teaspoon pepper
1/4 teaspoon Worcestershire sauce
2 cups milk
2 cups shredded Cheddar cheese

Heat oven to 350°

Melt butter in saucepan over low heat. Stir in flour, salt, mustard, pepper and Worcestershire sauce. Cook over low heat, stirring constantly, until mixture is smooth and bubbly; remove from heat. Stir in milk. Bring to a simmer, stirring constantly. Simmer, stirring, 1 minute; remove from heat. Stir in cheese. Fold pasta into cheese sauce. Spoon into sprayed or greased baking dish or individual ramekins.

Bake uncovered 20 to 25 minutes or until bubbly.

Red Flannel Hash

2 Tablespoons butter combined
with two Tablespoons canola oil
1 cup chopped onion
2 cups chopped cooked corned beef
1 1/2 cups chopped cooked beets
1 1/2 cups chopped cooked potatoes
1/4 cup (packed) chopped fresh parsley
Freshly ground black pepper to taste

Heat butter and oil in a frying pan on medium high. Add the onions and cook until translucent – three minutes. Combine corned beef, potatoes and beets and spread out evenly in the pan. Reduce the heat to medium. Press down with a spatula to help brown the mixture. Cook without stirring until golden brown on one side, then with your spatula, lift up sections of the mixture and turn over to brown the other side. Add a little more butter/oil to the pan if it's sticking.

When golden brown on both sides, remove from heat. Sprinkle on chopped parsley and pepper to taste. Corned Beef is already salty, so be conservative! Serve plain or with fried or poached eggs on top.

1963

January 12, 1963

Dear Tournier,

Geez, Junior, I think everyone else should call you Tournier, and
everyone has to call me Glory except you, and Uncle Jon, I guess, since
he started it– you can still call me Chief. In private. Only. Or, maybe... T
and G?

I accidentally put the sewing machine needle through my finger
yesterday, which hurt like the dickens, especially when I had to pull
it out, and Gloria says I never should have been in the Home Ec room
by myself, so she is really mad at the nuns for not monitoring me
more carefully. Shoot, Gloria doesn't know that Susie Jones and I, the
two not-Catholics in the entire student body, greased the doorknob
to the Music room the other day and shimmied out the window to
walk downtown in the snow while everyone else was in Religion class.
I wonder if Sister Helen is sorry she ever let two heathens into the
school. She kind of had to in my case, since Pop is one of her best
friends. But, still...

Anyway, I am home today from school, nursing my throbbing finger,
so I am typing with three fingers instead of four (flunked typing class
just like writing with my right hand). Gloria is making me a Puffy
Omelet, which is like a soufflé but cooked on the stove instead of in the
oven, and Bacon (I wish Marnie were here – she'd be happy to have
something to put maple syrup on.)

G

Puffy Omelet

3 egg whites
3 egg yolks
3 Tablespoons milk
salt and pepper
1 Tablespoon butter

sour cream and chopped tomatoes

Beat the egg whites until stiff. Beat egg yolks until thick. Beat milk into egg yolks and add salt and pepper. Fold the beaten egg whites into the egg yolk and milk mixture. Heat butter in skillet and gently pour egg mixture in. (Gloria liked to let the butter brown a little – it adds a distinctive flavor to the omelet). Cook omelet in skillet on low heat about ten minutes until the bottom is browned slightly. Carefully turn the omelet over and continue cooking until golden on this side.

Or, you can cook it a little longer on the first side, sprinkle some cheese in and simple fold it over like a regular omelet. Both of these methods take some flipping skill. An alternative is to finish it off in a 350° oven to brown the top. Serve with sour cream and chopped tomatoes or other topping or sauce. Or plain. Or with maple syrup. Really.

March 20, 1964

Dear T,

Well, I guess all those Junior Assembly dance classes are going to
finally pay off. Gloria said I could go to the Cotillion, since Martin is
going to escort his sweetheart, Virginia Bloom, for her "coming out"
on March 30th – when she will be presented to society and all those
marriageable bachelors, which is weird, 'cause Martin might have
something to say about that...

Gloria made my dress - a gold lace skirt over gold taffeta with gold
velvet bodice and a big gold velvet bow at the back. Gloria made it! And
gold-lace high heels! My first real high heels!! Whoa!

Virginia will be in white, of course, with all the other debutantes. White
Shoes. White Kid gloves to her elbows with teeny little pearl buttons all
the way up.

One of Martin's classmates from Kitchener, Tom Henderson, is my date.
He'll be in a tux!

So, the night before the Big Night we are hosting a dinner party for
Virginia at our house. We are dressing up, but not like above. Besides, I
am going to help Gloria and Mildred first.

Since Gloria and I are concentrating on French cooking right now,
she's going all out for this dinner party. She bought a copy of **Larousse
Gastronomique** and some French cookbooks and has been all crazy
with sauces and is calling Aunt Verna all the time for Mama Tournier's
recipes.

See, this Junior Assemblies thing?... is all about manners. Those old
ladies taught us how to dance and all (hold each other at arms length,
don't let your bodies touch, look over his left shoulder at something
else... ha ha), but all this other stuff comes into play now. I know that
the whole idea of a ball is in honor of the girl, Virginia in our case, being
ready to make her debut in society - but she couldn't do it at a barn
dance? A sock hop? No, no, we have to have a chance to prove to our
parents that we were listening!

-forks on the left, spoons and knives on the right (did you know that a blade pointed out means you wish the person across from you harm? Really. In 1660 or so in France, Cardinal Richelieu made all table knives rounded to keep people from jumping up in an argument and slashing at each other!)

-silver is set so you can "begin from the outside and work in" - fish fork, salad fork, main course fork, blah blah...

-bread and rolls are broken into bite-sized pieces and butter is spread on each bite as you nibble.

Which makes me think: why do they call eating with other people "breaking bread"? That's it!

The dictionary says that the words "company" and "companion" come from the latin "com," meaning "with" or "together," and "panis," which means "bread" or "food." Companions are the people you like to break bread with!

Gloria gave me this hilarious book about Etiquette written in 1925 - there's this girl, Gladys, and her mother, Mrs. Algernon Coutant, who are hosting a Cotillion Tea Dance. Here's the first paragraph:

Features of the Debutante Tea with Dancing - The elaborate decorative scheme which is often a feature of a debutante ball falls away in the tea with dancing. A background of flowers where Gladys stands, some palms to hide the musicians, are all that is needed. The debutante, Gladys, receives with her mother. Curtains are drawn and lights lighted as though for an evening ball, whether the tea with dancing be given in the home or at assembly rooms of some kind. Rain calls for an awning and a carpet when the affair is given at home. A doorman or chauffeur opens motor doors, and the butler (or a caterer's man) opens the house door. No guest should have to ring. Guests are announced on arrival, and Mrs. Coutant and her daughter, Gladys, receive as at a debutante ball. The younger set is free to dance as soon as the hostess has been greeted. The seniors sit about, drink tea and converse.

No guest should have to ring! When I am a senior, will I "sit about?"

Seriously,

G

Here's our menu - I wrote 8 of them out by hand with felt tip markers for each place setting – Virginia's parents, my parents, Martin and Virginia, Tom and me... Is this my first date? And does it count since I know him really well already? And worse, that he's my brother's best friend?

Cotillion Dinner for Eight

Brie and paté and crackers

•

Coquilles St. Jacques

•

Fresh, Crisp Salad Greens
with French Vinaigrette

•

Boeuf Bourguignon

•

French Bread

•

Mousseline au Chocolat

Coquille St. Jacques

2 pounds bay scallops
2 small onions, sliced
1 lemon, sliced
1 bay leaf
1 cup dry white wine
1 cup water
6 Tablespoons unsalted butter
4 Tablespoons minced shallots
1 teaspoon minced garlic
2 cup wild (if possible) mushrooms, sliced
4 Tablespoons flour
1 cup milk
2 teaspoons fresh lemon juice
1 teaspoon salt
1 teaspoon pepper
pinch cayenne
4 Tablespoons minced parsley
4 Tablespoons green onions, minced
1 cup heavy cream
1 cup shredded Gruyere

1 cup fine dry bread crumbs
2 Tablespoon melted butter
1/2 cup grated Parmesan

Preheat the broiler. Lightly butter the insides of 8 large scallop shell baking dishes or ramekins and place on 2 baking sheets that have been covered with parchment. Set aside. In a large sauté pan, combine scallops, onions, lemon, bay leaf, wine, and water. Bring to a simmer and gently poach the scallops until just firm, about 3 minutes. Remove scallops with a slotted spoon and reserve on a plate. Strain the poaching liquid into a clean bowl.

In a clean sauté pan, melt 1 tablespoon of the butter over medium-high heat. Add the shallots and garlic, and cook, stirring, for 30 seconds. Add the mushrooms and cook, stirring, until tender, about 4 minutes. Remove with a slotted spoon.

Add the remaining 2 tablespoons of butter to the pan the mushrooms were cooked in, and melt over medium heat. Make a light roux by adding the flour and cooking, stirring constantly for 2 minutes. Add the strained poaching liquid, stirring constantly, and cook until thick, about 2 minutes. Add the milk, lemon juice, salt, pepper, and cayenne, and whisk well. Bring to a boil and cook for 1 minute. Add the parsley and green onions, and simmer for 1 minute. Add the cream and Gruyere, stir well, and remove from the heat. Fold in the scallops and mushrooms, and pour into the prepared ramekins.

At this point, the scallops may be set-aside at room temperature for 1/2 hour while other menu items are prepped.

In a small bowl, combine the breadcrumbs and butter. Sprinkle over the scallop mixture and top with the Parmesan. Place under the broiler until just crisp and brown, 1 to 2 minutes. Remove from the heat and serve on a plate draped with a napkin to hold the heat.

French Vinaigrette

1/8 teaspoon sea salt
1 Tablespoon sherry wine vinegar
1/2 small shallot, peeled and minced
1/2 teaspoon Dijon mustard
4 Tablespoons olive oil

In a small jar, mix together the salt, vinegar, and shallot.

Let stand for about ten minutes.

Mix in the Dijon mustard, add olive oil. Shake well.

Boeuf Bourguignon

6 ounces of bacon, cut into small pieces
1 Tablespoon olive oil
3 1/2 pounds beef rump roast
flour for dredging beef
2 onions
2 carrots
3 Tablespoons flour
2 Tablespoons butter
2 Tablespoons olive oil
1 small can tomato paste
2 garlic cloves,
peeled and crushed
3 cups burgundy wine
2 cups beef stock*
1 bouquet garni
(parsley, thyme, bay)
salt & pepper

Simmer bacon pieces in water for ten minutes. Drain and dry.
In a 10 inch pot, sauté bacon in olive oil for a few minutes to brown
lightly. Remove with slotted spoon to small plate.

Prepare and cut the beef in 2 inch pieces and toss in flour in a paper or
plastic bag. Add the butter to the bacon fat and brown the meat. When
browned, sprinkle with the 3 Tablespoons flour and pour in the wine to
cover. Add tomato paste, crushed garlic and bouquet garni and season
with salt & pepper. Cover and simmer for 2 to 3 hours.

Peel carrots and onions and cut into thin slices. Add to simmering pot.
Simmer uncovered an additional hour, or until carrots and onions are
tender. When meat is tender, if the sauce is too liquid, take the meat and
vegetables out, then reduce it for a few minutes. Then put the meat and
vegetables back in. And the Bacon. Can be set aside for up to several days
and reheated – slowly. Serve.

Honey Baby Darlin' Book One - The Farm, page 118

Basic Table Manners

... are mostly common sense. From a Formal Dinner
to a Luncheon Bridge Party (does anyone here play Bridge?), these are really...basic.

1. **Sit up straight.** *Don't slouch or tip your chair back. At the least, it insults the host, at the worst, you might fall over backwards and crack your head.*

2. **Don't talk with your mouth full of food.** *Mother was right – again. No one wants to see the chewed food in your mouth.*

3. **Chew quietly, and don't slurp your soup.** *This follows #2 for a reason. Making noises is unappetizing, distracting, and interrupts the flow of conversation.*

4. **Take small bites.** *Don't shovel the food into your mouth – it's unattractive and tends to hang out of your mouth in transit.*

5. **Eat slowly.** *Better for digestion and respects your host and other guests; you know, like, makes them think you actually want to be there with them instead of home knitting.*

6. **Don't gesture with your utensils:** *like a knife with the tendrils of meat hanging from it. You might knock something over or fling food at someone.*

7. **Keep your elbows off the table.** *Yeah, yeah, mother again. Elbow-leaning makes you slouch.*

8. **Don't Reach.** *You don't want to get in the way or drag your sleeve through the soup. Ask for things to be passed. Oh, and when someone asks you to pass the salt, always keep the salt and pepper together – they are partners on the table dance.*

9. **Remember please and thank you.** *Common courtesy everywhere, but at the table, especially!*

10. **Excuse yourself when leaving the table.** *Let people think you are sooo sad to leave them but, pressing, urgent matters give you no other recourse...*

11. **Compliment the Cook.** *Say something nice, even if you've hidden your inedible sauerkraut or sneaked the overcooked meat to the hungry dog at your feet.. Don't lie, just think of something good to say, like, "Gee, that was really interesting Couscous."*

12. **Don't leave a lipstick smear on your glass.** *Wipe your lips with your napkin before drinking.*

A few more DON'Ts:

Don't:
- *begin eating before a signal from the host to do so*
- *pick your teeth*
- *drink too much*
- *lick your fingers*
- *slide peas onto your knife*

Mousseline au Chocolat

heat proof mixing bowl
4 egg yolks
3/4 cup bakers' sugar
1/4 cup orange liqueur
pan of water, simmering
bowl of cold water

6 ounces semi-sweet baking chocolate
4 Tablespoons coffee
6 ounces softened unsalted butter

4 egg whites
pinch of salt

Beat yolks and sugar until thick and pale yellow, until it forms "ribbons,"
about eight minutes. Add orange liqueur. Set bowl over hot water and
beat again until foamy and hot. Place over the cold water and beat again
to thick ribbon stage.

Melt chocolate and coffee over hot water. Remove from heat and beat in
the butter, a little at a time, until creamy. Beat the chocolate mixture into
the yolk mixture.

Beat egg whites with salt to form soft peaks. Fold egg whites into
chocolate mixture, one half at a time. Turn out into serving dish,
ramekins, champagne glasses, or some other individual serving
container. Serve with whipped cream or Crème Anglaise.*

** Recipe Page 183*

February 23, 1964
Dear Diary,

Whoa! I had a date! Well, I guess you could call it a date. The Cotillion was sooooo cooool. We danced til midnight, ate little sandwiches (had to remove my gloves!) and drank punch til 2am!

Tom is a very good dancer, which is great, because I danced with several boys (on my dance card! another thing to write T about! A full dance card!) who weren't so good at dancing as he is. Virginia pretty much glowed in white - her dress trailed behind her like Queen Elizabeth, little rhinestones sparkling in puddles of white satin. Martin and Tom were dashing in their tuxedos! I never realized Tom was so handsome. He wasn't the regular ol' guy I've known forever. I think he thought the same of me. We had some awkward moments.

The ballroom was filled with palms (yes! Palms! But, they didn't hide the musicians, for which James was grateful) and other giant plants and the whole place was flooded with soft candlelight.

Everyone was on their best behavior - sooo appropriate. Sooo.... oh, say it, Glory, boring. This is your diary, after all. Who's going to see this? My dress was beautiful, but, as always, I couldn't wait to get home and get out of it! Jeans and shirts for this girl! I can't help it. Gloria despairs over me. Every time I went to the ladies room to hike up my pantyhose, she criticized me like Emily Post. I argued that when Emily Post was writing, pantyhose had not been invented.

It wasn't a kissing kind of date or anything, because Tom says I am too young (please – I am 15) and besides, I am his best friend's little sister (puhlease!). He said Martin made him promise to "be good."

I'll make a lousy deb.

April, 1964

Dear T,

The Players' Guild sponsored the Spring Sock Hop to raise money for our next production. We decorated the gym to look like a Bedouin tent! Everyone brought rugs and lamps and pillows and stuff. It was cool.

We had snacks!

Here's what we served on big silver platters:

Dates stuffed with cream cheese
Flatbreads with yogurt sauce and chickpea "paste"
Sheep and goat cheese with pita "crackers"
Olives
Walnut cookies
Baklava
Cokes and root beer (not too Bedouin...)

Gloria and I made the Baklava! There is a lot of Phyllo and melted butter-slathering in the process, but it was fun.

We decided to forego the native costumes – too ... mmm... too trip-able for dancing DJ style.

Enclosed in this box are some Baklava and Walnut cookies.

Chief

P.S. I jitterbugged with Seamus Ireland from St. Luke's.

Bedouin Bread

1 Tablespoon active dry yeast
1 Tablespoon honey
1 1/4 cups tepid water
3 1/2 cups flour
1 teaspoon salt

Dissolve yeast and honey in water. Sift in the flour and salt. Mix well and knead lightly on a floured board. Cut dough into 8 pieces and shape into rounds.

Roll until 5 inches across and 1/4 inch thick. Place on lightly greased cookie sheet, cover with a clean towel and let rise in a warm place for an hour or two.

Preheat oven to 500°

Let rise to thickness of about 1/2 inch. Bake for 7 to 8 minutes.

Walnut Cookies

2 cups semolina flour
1 1/2 cups melted butter
1 cup boiling water
1 teaspoon orange blossom essence
1 teaspoon rose water
3/4 cup fine sugar
1 1/4 cups crushed walnuts

Make dough from semolina, butter and boiling water and knead well.
Cover tightly with plastic wrap and leave overnight. On second day:
Preheat oven to 350°. Knead dough and form into small balls. Hollow
out centers of balls. Mix together sugar, nuts and essences. Fill hollows
with mixture. Press dough back over the filling. Press each cookie onto a
buttered baking pan and flatten.

Bake at 350° until lightly browned. Dust with powdered sugar while
warm.

Baklava

1 pound walnuts,
coarsely chopped
2 ounces sugar
1 teaspoon cinnamon
1 pound phyllo pastry
6 Tablespoons unsalted butter,
melted
1 cup sugar
1 1/4 cups water
2 cinnamon sticks
2 teaspoons lemon juice
1 Tablespoon lemon peel
2 Tablespoons honey
(optional)

Mix all filling ingredients in a bowl. Butter base and sides of a 9 x 12 inch baking dish. Cut phyllo to length of baking dish with a sharp knife.

Preheat oven to 350°. Place each layer of phyllo in buttered pan, brush with melted butter and place evenly around the bottom of the baking dish. After 5 layers of phyllo, spread a thin layer of filling over the Repeat with phyllo and filling, ending with phyllo on the top – 4-5 layers.

Fold any excess pastry on either of the sides over the filling and brush it all over with butter. Brush the top layer liberally with butter. Trim any excess pastry with a small sharp knife, but remember it shrinks. Sprinkle drops of water all over the top surface and bake for 30 minutes, until golden.

Place all syrup ingredients, except honey, in a saucepan and stir to dissolve sugar. Simmer for 6-8 minutes, add honey and simmer for 5 minutes until it thickens. Pour hot, not boiling syrup slowly all over the baklava (use a strainer) and let it stand to absorb all the syrup. Let cool and cut into pieces.

September 1, 1964
Dear T,

Well, it's official. Seamus Ireland and I are going steady. He gave
me his St. Luke's class ring, which is too big for me, so I wear it
around my neck on a chain.

Gloria and James aren't too happy, because they think he is
"moving too fast." Pop thinks he is too much from a different
world (he's a crazy, middle-class Irish boy whose mother raised
two kids by herself after his father died when he was little) and
Martin says he'll smack him if he isn't nice to me.

Well, so far he is nice to me, he can dance, he has a car and he
plays soccer and football, which is intriguing, since no one in my
family is in to sports. He's Irish, duh.

And, yes, he has kissed me, but I didn't tell any of those people
mentioned above.

I am applying to Endicott Junior College, to make Gloria happy.
GB

*"You should wipe your spoon before
passing it to a neighbor."*

*"Do not blow your nose with the same
hand that you use to hold the meat."*

-- Erasmus, Dutch humanist
and author of the first modern
book of manners for children in 1526.

September 10, 1964
Dear Diary,

Last night we had a Texas BBQ for the ten kids in my Teen Thespian group at the Community Players. James put on his old Kiss the Cook apron, which has seen better days – I think it's time for a new one – and made Spareribs and Burgers with Texas BBQ sauce. It was cool but messy, which I guess BBQ sauce is supposed to be, if it's really good. James said it should drip all over your hands, which it absolutely did.

4 pounds pork or beef ribs,
cut into single serving pieces
about 4 ribs each hungry person
3 cups water
¼ cup soy sauce
2 Tablespoons cornstarch

Put ribs and water in a large pot with a cover. Bring to a simmer and cook five minutes. Remove ribs and drain on paper towel. Mix soy sauce with cornstarch and place in a shallow pan. Place ribs in pan and turn occasionally to coat ribs with marinade. Leave in marinade for about an hour.

Cook ribs on a greased grill over hot coals or high (gas) heat for about 30 minutes, turning frequently and basting with **Texas BBQ Sauce**. Serve with remaining sauce.

Texas BBQ Sauce

3 cups tomato juice
1/2 cup ketchup
1 cup water
1/4 cup balsamic vinegar
3 Tablespoons brown sugar
1 teaspoon mustard
(dry or from a jar)
1/4 teaspoon chili powder
salt and pepper

Mix ingredients together and simmer in a saucepan for about 20 minutes, or until thickened. Makes about 3 cups.

Graduation, 1965
Dear Diary,

Oh. Oh.

Uh oh. Seamus and I are about to face some serious music. $%*&'@#$!

Everything just going along, and boom.

My world is being crushed. How did this happen to me? No, I know how it happened. That's not what I mean.

With a snap of the fingers - just like that! Everything is changing.

Oh, oh, oh. I can't bear the disappointment in my mother's eyes.

Oh God.

Author's Note:

Glory stops rifling through the box of memorabilia marked "**60s**." She searches for the next diary entry, the next letter, clipped recipe, scribbled note that will move her forward in her story about cooking and all its... uhm... glory... and realizes there is a gap. A big gap. She collates and rifles some more. She searches for the key, the clue, the word.

It's amazing, the grown-up Glory says aloud to her Muse. More than 18 months... phfft. Where did it go? What was I doing? Was I there or did I just imagine it? Who did that? Why didn't I write anything down?

Whoa, says Madame La Muse. You fell in so-called teenage love. You bagged your lofty plans and went careening off onto the stormy sea with your supposed hero. Methinks the sea was too choppy for you...

Hmmmm, thinks Glory. No kidding. No recipes there except for disaster. If it seems abrupt, it was. One minute life was promising a future, the next, I was in despair.

So, Glory distills in her memory those lost months-

heartache, diapers
pizza, beer
cigarettes, fire
abandonment, teeth hurt
apartment a mess- squalor
dreams shattered
hopes trashed
baby loved
tears shed
back patted
floor walked
boyfriend/husband a disappointment
parents reflecting
hurting...
moving...
leaving...
saving...
escape.

Part Two
1967-1980

January 12, 1967

Dear T,

I never should have married Seamus. This has been a big mistake. We are not compatible. We are like serving Hot and Sour Soup over ice cream; we're a Bluegrass Fiddle player and a ballroom dancer caught together in a barbed wire fence; a bag of raccoons; a bathtub full of alligators; a bookworm and a sports nut. Besides, he doesn't want or know how to be a father.

I think I fell off the earth into some alternate reality. Sorry I have not written in a while, but I am in a deep bowl of **Flossie's Spaghetti** here and it might as well be quicksand.

Thank God Gloria is a safe distance away in her new digs in California and does not know the scope of my failure as a surprised mommy, young wife, and cook.

Flossie comes to visit us in our little flat (I force my jumbled mess into the closet – like Fibber Mcgee's at Wistful Vista!). She brings **Pineapple Upside-Down Cake** and sits for an hour with a quiet, burbling little Billy on her expansive lap. "Billy Ireland," she'll say, "give your old Flossie a big kiss," and he'll tug at her turban and plant a big wet one on her ruby lips, usually while digging in her purse for a treat.

They are in love, my Billy and Flossie. I know we'll both miss the lilt in her voice when we have to go.

Please come visit.

G

25 ripe but firm Roma tomatoes,
chopped
4 Tablespoons olive oil
1 onion, chopped
2 carrots, chopped
2 stalks celery
4 cloves garlic,
minced
1/4 cup chopped fresh basil
1/4 teaspoon Italian seasoning
1/4 cup burgundy
or other full-bodied red wine
1 bay leaf
2 Tablespoons tomato paste

Cook onion, carrot, celery and garlic in oil until onion softens, about 5 minutes. Stir in chopped tomato, basil, Italian seasoning, wine and bay leaf. Cover and simmer 2 hours. Stir in tomato paste and simmer an additional 2 hours. Discard bay leaf and serve over cooked pasta.

Pineapple Upside-down Cake

Preheat oven to 375°

10" iron skillet
1 can pineapple slices, drained, reserve juice
1 cup brown sugar
1/4 cup unsalted butter
1/2 cup maple syrup
1/2 cup chopped pecans

4 Tablespoons unsalted butter
1 cup milk
2 cups organic, unbleached white flour
1 Tablespoon baking powder
4 eggs
2 cups sugar
2 Tablespoons vanilla

In skillet, reduce juice to heavy syrup. Add brown sugar, butter and maple syrup and melt together. Sprinkle with nuts. Place pineapple slices into skillet on top of mixture. Set aside.

In heavy saucepan, warm milk and butter until butter is just melted. Set aside to cool. Sift together flour and baking powder. Beat eggs in mixer at high speed until thick ribbons are formed, about seven minutes. Gradually fold in sugar and vanilla. Slowly add dry ingredients alternately with cooled milk/butter mixture (this mixture must be cooled so as not to deflate eggs), ending with dry ingredients. Pour over nut and pineapple mixture in skillet.

Bake at 375° for about 40 minutes or until golden and slightly firm. Cool ten minutes. Turn upside-down on platter. Makes ten pieces.

Wichita, Kansas
April, 1967
Dear T,

Thanks for the sisterly pep-talk. And thanks for not giving me a hard
time about leaving Seamus and helping me pack instead.

James and Gloria had a collective and predictable fit when they heard
my intentions, first of my "impulsive escape" from this ridiculous
marriage (the words "impulsive escape" theirs, "ridiculous marriage,"
mine.) - "You made your bed – you should lie in it" Gloria said – they
just don't understand that the sheets don't fit the marriage bed, or
maybe they DO understand, which was why they didn't approve of the
whole thing in the first place. By the time I called them, I had already
said goodbye to Seamus Ireland, avoiding that big jagged chip on his
hot-tempered shoulder, placed the doomed-from-the-start teenaged
marriage in my rearview mirror and was on my way to California – I
guess "going home" is wherever my folks are.

I parked at Sky-Way Drive-In to map out my route and ordered a
chocolate shake to entertain Billy Ireland, drying my tears with first
my sleeve and then the brown wrapper of my Cheeseburger, none of
Marnie's lady-like hankies being close at hand. My stomach was in the
pretzel-knot of flight - I think the burger is still under the front seat of
the car.

When James gave me the precious Woody for graduation in '65, telling
me to "have it serviced regularly and to take good care of it, dammit,
that thing's a prize," did he think for a minute that I would be driving it
back to California on my own – ah, well, me and my beautiful little high
school graduation present?

Rearing a Child
James Baker

You know more
Than you think you know
About what it takes
For a child to grow

Rearing a child is
Really a pleasure
If common sense is
Abundant in measure

Instinct and
Certain amounts of emotion
Combined with good sense
And lots of devotion

to T, continued...

Right now we are with Aunt Verna, in her Victorian hobbit house in
Wichita, Kansas – Billy and me, my red typewriter perched on one
of Aunt Verna's dainty and rickety doily-covered antique tables that
should probably be holding nothing heavier than a very thin porcelain
tea cup, and the Marx brothers, her four cocker spaniels: Groucho,
Harpo, Zeppo and Karl.

Billy is asleep, sprawled across the tiny horse-hair sofa (everything
here is tiny, except Aunt Verna) with his thumb in his mouth and
Zeppo, or is it Karl?, curled up by his feet. Aunt Verna (who's gone
to bed so she can get up at 5 to go to the Swim Gym) gave me a box
of raggedy sepia photos and an old recipe book to look at – written
in Mama Tournier's own handwriting and fractured English. About
French Pastry. Did you know that Aunt Verna is 80 (she is the oldest of
eight – Marnie the youngest), plays bridge at her club every day, drives
a 1950 turquoise convertible Peugeot with the back seat removed for
the cockers and goes swimming twice a week? Her miniscule closet
smells like lavender, her bathroom of chlorine (there is a frilly, skirted
bathing suit hanging on the back of the door!), her house, other than
the four hairy dog beds in front of the fire, is spotless and the kitchen
filled with gleaming copper pots, which, of course, I covet. She still
makes her own stock. Marnie was the only sister who was not inspired
by the art of cooking. Abundance is written all over Verna. Like Flossie.
From ample bosom to sturdy shoes.

During Flossie's last visit, I asked her how it felt to leave the Farm to
retire and also say goodbye to Bessie when she married Clarke and
moved to Louisiana. Flossie said, "Uh, uh, huh! I sho' do miss dat gal.
We like family - like you. Dey was good years, at de Farm."

Yes. All that's gone now. Everything is new. When I said goodbye to
Flossie and watched her 75-year-old-self drive off in that antediluvian
black Cadillac, I didn't even let myself entertain the idea until
yesterday, driving across Missouri, that I might not see her or Lincoln
again. She gave me her Farm recipe books and picture albums, and a
quilt she and Lincoln made of "Farm stuff"- dungarees and plaid shirts,
muslin aprons, army blankets. She has one for you.

And, I'll miss you, too, but I blinked back tears in your arms. I know I'll
see you in California. I will, right? And I'll come back for your wedding.

More from on the road... I'll call when I have enough dimes. Aunt Verna
is going to teach me how to make Puff Pastry!!! From scratch! She says
it doesn't really take three days.

Glory

**Flossie's
Chili & "Cheesy-cakes"**

Cheesy-cakes

1 1/2 cups all-purpose flour
2 teaspoons double-acting
baking powder
1/2 teaspoon baking soda
1/2 teaspoon salt
2 Tablespoons cold unsalted butter,
cut into bits
1/4 pound sharp Cheddar,
grated coarse
(about 1 1/2 cups)
4 2-inch pickled jalapeño chilies,
seeded and minced
(rubber gloves
are good protection)
1 cup sour cream

Preheat oven to 425°

Sift together flour, baking powder, baking soda and salt, add butter, and
blend until it resembles coarse meal. Stir in Cheddar and chilies, add
sour cream, and stir until it forms a soft but not sticky dough. Knead on
a lightly floured surface and roll out 1/2 inch thick. With a 3 1/2-inch
biscuit cutter, cut out 6 pieces. Bake on a parchment-covered baking
sheet for 12 minutes.

The Chili

2 large onions, chopped (about 3 cups)
3 carrots, chopped
3 stalks celery, chopped
1/4 cup vegetable oil
1 Tablespoon minced garlic
3 pounds ground beef chuck
1/4 cup chili powder
1 Tablespoon ground cumin
1 Tablespoon crumbled dried oregano
1 Tablespoon dried hot red pepper flakes, or to taste
2 8-ounce cans tomato sauce
1 1/4 cups beef stock
2 19-ounce can kidney beans, rinsed and drained
extra shredded Cheddar cheese
cilantro

Sauté the onions, carrots and celery in the oil over moderately low heat, stirring occasionally, until softened, add garlic, cook, stirring, for about 1 minute. Add the ground beef and cook over moderate heat, stirring and breaking up any lumps, for 10 minutes, or until cooked through. Add chili powder, cumin, oregano, and red pepper flakes and cook for 1 minute. Add the tomato sauce, stock, and vinegar, bring to a boil, simmer, covered, stirring occasionally, for 50 minutes to 1 hour, or until the meat is tender. Add the kidney beans, salt and black pepper to taste and simmer uncovered for 15 minutes.

Place chili in individual serving bowls, with a Cheesy-cake on top. Sprinkle with grated cheese and cilantro.

Mama Tournier's
French Puff Pastry

Butter Dough

2 cups flour
16 Tablespoons unsalted butter
2/3 cup ice cold water

Mix 1/4 cup of flour with 14 tablespoons of cold butter to make a smooth paste. Shape into a square about 1/2 inch x 4 inches. Cover and refrigerate 30 minutes.

Water-Based Dough

(the *détrempe* – meaning sodden or water-logged!)

Separately, mix the cold water, 2 tablespoons of butter, and the remaining 1-3/4 cup of flour (add 1/4 teaspoon of salt here, optional). Knead for one minute. Cover and refrigerate 30 minutes to relax the gluten - this helps to roll out the dough without it crumbling or breaking apart.

On a lightly floured board, roll out the *détrempe* to a thickness of 3/8 inch. Place the butter dough in the middle of the water-based dough and wrap the ends of the water-based dough over the butter dough to enclose it, as in an envelope. Roll out the dough envelope to 3/8 inch thickness and fold in thirds, like a business letter. Roll again in the opposite direction and fold in thirds again.

Refrigerate 30 minutes and repeat the process twice for a total of six folding-over. As the dough is folded into thirds, the layers are tripled, so after six times there are 729 dough layers and 729 butter layers.

The secret of good puff pastry: *always work the dough while cold to prevent the butter and water-based dough from mixing. This is how to retain the layered structure. So, the cooling periods are key:* if the dough warms it will soften the butter and blend it with the *détrempe*. After the sixth folding-over, the dough is refrigerated again, and is then ready for use.

Another secret to good pastry of any sort*: Always preheat the oven to at least 400°. If your oven isn't hot enough, the butter melts and the moisture evaporates before steam forms to separate the layers, which creates a tough pastry.*

Rough Puff Pastry
somewhat easier – no butter dough involved

1 1/4 cups all-purpose flour
1/4 teaspoon salt
1 stick (1/2 cup) plus 5 tablespoons
unsalted butter, frozen
5 to 6 tablespoons ice water

In a chilled large metal bowl, sift together flour and salt. Coarsely grate frozen butter into the flour with a grater. Gently toss mixture to coat the butter with the flour.

Drizzle 5 tablespoons ice water evenly over flour mixture and gently stir with a fork until incorporated. Test mixture by gently squeezing a small handful: if it has the proper texture, it will hold together without crumbling. Add another tablespoon water, stirring until just incorporated and testing again, if necessary. (Don't overwork the mixture or add too much water or the pastry will be tough.)

Gather the mixture together and form into a square of about six inches, then chill, wrapped in plastic wrap, until firm, about 30 minutes. (Dough will be lumpy and streaky with butter.)

Roll out dough on a floured surface with a floured rolling pin into a 15-by- 8-inch rectangle. Arrange dough with a short side nearest you, then fold dough into thirds like a letter: bottom third up and top third down over dough. Rewrap dough and chill until firm, about 30 minutes.

Arrange dough with a short side nearest you on a floured surface and repeat rolling out, folding, and chilling 2 more times. Brush off any excess flour, then wrap dough in plastic wrap and chill at least 1 hour.

Palmiers

Roll out the dough to a thickness of 1/8 inch. Sprinkle with superfine sugar so the whole sheet of dough is lightly covered. Roll two opposite edges of the dough toward the middle to make a log in a sort of heart shape. Cut log into slices about 1/4 inch thick. Place the slices on a cookie sheet spaced about one inch apart. Bake at 425° for 8 minutes or until golden brown.

Napoleons

A Napoleon is a *mille-feuille* ("thousand-leaf") in France - several layers of puffed pastry alternating with pastry cream. It's a lot more than a thousand leaves, if you count each sheet of 729 layers of dough and 729 layers of butter, and you have, say, four layers of puff pastry – that makes 2,916 layers of dough and 2,916 layers of butter, for a total of 5,832 "leaves." Impressive.

Roll out the puff pastry dough to 1/8 inch thickness and cut into equal rectangles or squares. Place the pieces on a parchment covered baking sheet and pierce with a fork to keep the dough from puffing too much. Bake at 450° F for approximately 7 minutes, or until the pastry is light brown. When cooled, add the filling and topping*, making several layers. Refrigerate and cut into serving pieces when cold.

*The Napoleons can be drizzled with chocolate, dusted with powdered sugar or topped with whipped cream.

Turnovers

Roll out the dough to a thickness of 1/8 in, cut into 4 inch squares, place a spoonful of fruit jam in each square and fold diagonally, pinching at the edges to create turnovers. Moisten the edges of the square before folding to stick them together when pressed with a fork. Pierce the turnover with a fork to allow steam to escape while baking. Brush the pastries with egg-wash and sprinkle with superfine sugar before baking for a rich golden color. Bake at 400° for 20 to 30 minutes until lightly browned.

Pastry Cream

4 cups whole milk
8 egg yolks
1 cup granulated sugar
10 Tablespoons cornstarch
1/8 teaspoon salt
3 teaspoons pure vanilla extract

In a saucepan, warm the milk over low heat until it steams. While the milk is warming, whisk together the egg yolks, sugar, cornstarch and salt until completely smooth.

Add half of the steamed milk, whisking constantly, to the egg mixture. Add the milk and eggs back into the rest of the hot milk, and heat for 1-2 minutes, stirring constantly, until the custard is very thick. Remove from the heat. Stir in the vanilla extract. Chill before filling pastry.

April 20, 1967

Dear Aunt Verna,

Thank you so much for five of the most wonderful days of my so far
little life. It wasn't just that you taught me how to make Puff Pastry, or
that Groucho, Harpo, Zeppo and Karl fell in love with Billy, and he with
them, or that you let us clutter up your living room for so long. Nor was
it that you put up with my clattering, furniture-bashing, note-churning
little red typewriter. It was all those things and more.

You never dwelt on my troubles and you showed me something about
growing up, growing older with grace and verve and staying young
forever. Thank you for being a model for me.

Billy and I have landed in Palm Springs to spend a few days with Pop
before joining Gloria and James in Carmel. This has been the best
trip across the country, filling me with ideas, plans and your amazing
strawberry preserves. I hope I am like you when I grow up.

Love, Glory

Palm Springs, California
April 20, 1967

Dearest T,

We've been two weeks, nine states (Ohio, Indiana, Illinois, Missouri,
Kansas, Texas, New Mexico, Arizona and California), three motels,
Aunt Verna's tiny sofa (with the furry Marx brothers for pillows),
6,000 diapers and umpteen gas and food stops on the road. What an
adventure! We've mostly had fun and Billy has been a good companion
even if his conversation isn't very stimulating. We packed 20
Strawberry preserve-filled Puff Pastry Turnovers for the road from

Verna's! (By the way, I will probably never
make Puff Pastry from scratch again as
long as I live, but we did have fun with
Aunt Verna and I love the idea that there
are 729 layers of butter and 729 layers of
dough.) Here's a picture of me feeding Puff
Pastry to a chipmunk while having lunch
at a rest stop.

We arrived in Palm Springs yesterday to
visit Pop, who, you'll love this, is ensconced
at the Spa Hotel eating Shrimp Louie
and having daily massages by suntanned
masseuses. Our diets have improved, as
well as our sleeping arrangements!

I know he didn't approve of my, uhm,
alliance, with Seamus, but still... he dotes
on Billy, and, as I have seen the light and
come home to the flock, or whatever, he
has mostly forgiven me.

To think – I left Seamus Ireland's Chef
Boyardee Spaghetti Sauce, endless games of Euchre and a long list
of grievances for this. When Billy wiggled off his lap, Pop mapped his
version of my future. I ordered **Chicken Papaya Salad** and followed
Billy to the pool.

This hunky Hungarian Gypsy Lion Tamer/Trapeze Artist (really)
named Poncho was in a lounge chair. I mean his Speedo barely covered
his nether regions. His companion, Iago the German Shepherd Wonder
Dog, was stretched out beside him. The only available seat was to
Poncho's left, which I plopped into with not much grace. For the better
view of Billy in the wading pool. Really.

We talked about everything from the circus and wild animal training to
child rearing, world travel, Gypsy food and politics. Billy dripped water
all over Iago and Iago watched over Billy, just like Major babysat us
four cousins at the Farm.

Poncho's family lived and traveled in a caravan for
as long as – well, he says longer than his mother's
curly black, babushka'd hair. He grew up in the circus,
following his uncles onto the trapeze, and then his
father into the Big Wild Cat cage - and pretty much
proved it with pictures! Their Gypsy food was all
prepared outdoors, over an open fire! One-pot meals
and sausages and rice, whole fishes, large crusty
loaves of bread, flatbreads and roasted meats on a
spit. Very cool.

More later...

Shrimp Louie

1/4 cup mayonnaise
2 Tablespoons good quality chili sauce
1 Tablespoon Dijon mustard
1 Tablespoon fresh lemon juice
1 teaspoon grated lemon peel
Salt and pepper to taste

4 cups mixed baby greens
1 avocado, peeled, halved, pitted
1 dozen cooked extra-large shrimp (sautéed is best)
peeled and deveined
1 green onion, finely chopped

Blend mayonnaise, chili sauce, mustard, lemon juice and lemon peel with a whisk in small bowl. Wash and dry greens, then arrange on 2 chilled salad plates. Top with 1 avocado half, pit cavity side up. Fill avocado cavities with shrimp. Drizzle dressing over all; sprinkle with green onion.

Gypsy Stew

1 cup dried chickpeas -- soaked overnight
2 pounds pork sausages, cooked and cut in pieces
10 cups water
2 medium potatoes -- peeled and cubed
2 medium bay leaves
1 onion, chopped
3 cloves garlic, chopped
1/3 cup olive oil
1 Butternut squash, peeled and cubed
1 cup green beans
1 bunch Swiss chard, chopped
1/2 cup bread crumbs
1 ounce almonds
1/4 teaspoon saffron
salt and pepper -- to taste
1 Tablespoon red wine vinegar

Place soaked beans, sausages and water in pan. Bring to boil and simmer
for 1 hour. Add potatoes and bay leaves and cook for another 30 minutes.
Fry onion and garlic in oil until golden. Add onion mixture and squash
to the stew. Simmer for 15 minutes. Then add remaining vegetables
and simmer for another 15 minutes. Grind almonds and mix with
breadcrumbs. Then add to stew along with saffron. Season with salt and
pepper and simmer for 5 minutes. Stir in vinegar and serve.

Chicken Papaya Salad

2 whole skinless chicken breasts,
cooked and sliced into bite sized pieces
2 papayas, peeled, halved, seeded,
and cut into 1/2 inch pieces
1 bunch green onions, cut in 1/4 inch pieces

1/2 cup olive oil
2 Tablespoon rice wine vinegar
1 bunch fresh tarragon, stems discarded, leaves chopped
Romaine lettuce, washed, dried, chilled and cut into pieces

Toss first three ingredients. Blend dressing. Arrange lettuce on chilled
salad plates. Arrange chicken mixture on greens. Pour dressing over and
serve.

Carmel

So, T, continued...

Wow. Time flies when one is lolling by the pool next to a handsome
Gypsy. I ate salads and drank iced tea and made extravagant promises
for three days – to Pop regarding what I will do when I grow up (I have
a child! I'm 19! Aren't I grown up enough yet?) and to Poncho about
sitting by the pool with him in Timbuktu or an Island somewhere in the
Pacific or his grandmother's trailer park in Barcelona.

But I am a homing pigeon and was headed toward Gloria. Here's a
picture of us on the grounds of the Carmel Mission. Gloria's kitchen has
a window box of parsley and nasturtiums and this completely amazing
picture postcard view of the roof of the Mission and the Chapel cross.
Billy and I share a room with its own entrance, in the midst of Gloria's
rose bushes.

We arrived like two ragamuffins, both dropping into Gloria's arms. Until
I got here, I didn't really get what I had just done, I guess I was too busy
doing it – left a dismal, doomed, hopeless, horrible, depressing situation
and drove across the country, me and Billy. Adrenaline and momentum
just kept me going west. Seamus has his own stuff to work out.

I now get down to the business of my life. I am
trying to make going toward something rather
than running away.

G

California Journal
May, 1967

What I love about Carmel:

I walk to the post office, down tree-lined streets, past cottages and houses with shaded gardens and narrow paths to the kelp-strewn beach.

It's quiet - the sound of the surf, distant voices of children with wet, sandy feet running with dogs and throwing sticks.

The fog burns off and the sun shines down.

Cafés with espresso, fresh croissants or scones with thick purple jam.

The Bistro Blue-Cheese Burger. The Village Corner – locals sit outside by the fire-pit.

The shopkeepers on Ocean Avenue: sisters Moira, Dottie and Ruth, running Ruthie's Jewelry Shoppe together for forty years – they live several blocks away in the house they grew up in (and they are not spring chickens), don't own cars, have never been married and have walked to work since, like, forever!

Or Mr. Tochet at the Mercantile – he wears a red bow tie and Plus Fours with an ever-changing array of patterned suspenders – and dark argyle knee socks and penny loafers - every day. And Mr. Forrester, the stationer. His leather apron? 40 years old, at least, molded to the shape of... Mr. Forrester.

Andre's Café - tables on the sidewalk. Beautiful, Bohemian beatnik-ish people sit at the tables and smoke thin cigarettes and drink prodigious amounts of coffee. You can see by their outfits that they are artists or writers – the men wear berets and black turtlenecks or denim shirts and jeans belted with wide leather and shiny buckles. The women all look like Mary Travers.

There are poetry readings at the coffeehouse.

Bearded boys play bongos in Devendorf Park in the middle of town.

Gloria takes me for drives down the coast to "smell the sea" and walks around the Carmel Point to "peer at gardens, view Point Lobos."

When I first headed west, I was wrapped in a cloud. I was running from problems. Gloria always says "Don't run away from your problems, because you just take them with you." Hmmm... I guess she is right.

But, now that I am here, I feel more like I am moving forward into something. Carmel has charmed me and taken me in. In a few short weeks, I have friends, a bed in a nice room in my parents home, a crib for my boy and some hope for the future.

May, 1967

Dear T,

I am still living with James and Gloria, since I left Seamus with a
hastily packed bag of big ideas and arrived with a wallet full of moths,
after my extravagant trip across the country. Pop still thinks I am
on vacation and wants me to come home and help him run the Sugar
empire, but... no.

Seriously, can you see me selling Sugar Shave? Being a sales rep?
TYPING?

This isn't typing, it's writing!

Billy is doing well and we are settling into life in California. Carmel is
like a toy town – thatched-roof cottages right out of fairy tales, lots
of shade trees and north-side-of-the-house type gardens – ferns and
cineraria and foxgloves. No street lights. No sidewalks outside the
downtown area. Quiet. I think James' job and the move here were good
for my parents.

I am glad I came. I can breathe the air here. It is right.

I have enrolled for summer classes - Design, Ceramics, Sociology and
Spanish - at the Junior College. Gloria is taking the Spanish class with
me, so she can order Mexican food without embarrassing herself (I'll
have the anchilado, per yur favor...).

I am currently knee-deep in Mexican cooking, my new west coast
discovery and latest personal Food Festival. I must be feeling better
– I am cooking! And our Spanish teacher, Mr. Martinez, is coming
over tomorrow night to cook with us – he is bringing his wife and her
homemade tortillas and Cilantro Dressing.

No, I have not heard from Seamus. Not once. He's certainly busy with
his own self. I always new he was the "out of sight, out of mind" kind of
guy.

Glory

Salsa

6 ripe red tomatoes, chopped
1 red or 6 green onions, chopped
Jalapeno chilies to taste, finely chopped
Juice of 1/2 lemon
Cilantro to taste, chopped (optional)
salt and pepper to taste

Combine ingredients in a bowl and refrigerate until use. Will hold in refrigerator several days.

Mango (or Papaya or Peach) Salsa
To above recipe, add a chopped mango, papaya and/or 2 peaches

garlic & herb tortillas,
or any kind of good quality
flour tortillas,
cut in strips or wedges
canola oil
salt

In oil about three inches deep, using medium high heat, fry strips of flour tortillas until crispy and golden. Drain on paper towel or in a recycled brown paper bag. Salt to taste while still hot.

Enchilada Sauce

8 dried Ancho chilies
two gallons boiling water
1/3 cup canola oil
4 cups each, chopped:
carrots, onions, celery
2 -3 cloves garlic, chopped
about a gallon of veggie or chicken stock*
1/2-1 cup cornmeal
1/4 cup brown sugar
1-2 teaspoons ground cumin
salt and pepper to taste
oregano to taste, optional

Place dried chilies in boiling water and turn off the heat. Soak about three hours or overnight. Drain, cool, stem and seed the chilies. Leave the skins on.

Sauté vegetables in hot oil in large pot until soft. Add chilies and stock. Simmer 20 minutes. Blend with hand held Soup Blender. Thicken with cornmeal, season with brown sugar, cumin, salt and pepper. This makes a lot. Can be frozen in zip locks or plastic container.

*HBD Book One – The Farm pages 111 or 114

Margarita's Tortillas
Modern day tortilla making is a snap in the Food Processor.

3 cups unbleached,
organic white flour*
1 teaspoon salt
1 Tablespoon canola oil
1/4 to 1/2 cup water

Place flour, salt and oil in Food Processor. Slowly add water through hole in top while processing. When the dough starts to come away from the sides and form a ball, stop the processor. Scrape dough out of container, dust with flour and place in plastic wrap in the refrigerator for up to 24 hours. Dough can also be frozen and thawed completely before the next step.

Cut dough ball into approximately 12 equal pieces, roll into balls and dust with flour. Set aside. On a floured board, roll each ball into a round, shaping as you go. Tortilla rolling pins are handy - they are small, easy to use, and are curved at either end for easy shaping.

*For Corn Tortillas, substitute masa harina for the flour and use a bit more water. You can leave out the oil. Rolling corn tortillas is easiest between two wet towels or between sheets of parchment.

Keep tortillas under a wet towel as you flip them on a hot griddle or in a large frying pan, dry or with a small amount of oil to crisp.

My Guacamolé

2 ripe avocados, mashed
1 cup fresh or
thawed and drained frozen corn,
pan roasted
in oil or butter
and cooled
3 green onions, finely chopped
fresh cilantro, to taste, chopped
Juice of 1/2 lemon
salt to taste

Gently mix all ingredients. Keep pits in Guacamolé and/or spread lightly
with mayo to keep from turning brown. Refrigerate until ready to serve.
Does not keep well overnight.

Serve with Homemade Flour Tortilla Chips, page 111

Vegetarian Enchiladas

12 green onions, chopped
3 carrots, chopped
2 stalks celery, chopped
1 clove garlic, finely chopped
1 cup fresh or thawed and drained frozen corn,
pan roasted in oil or butter and cooled
3-4 cups grated cheddar cheese
1 small can sliced black olives, optional
½ teaspoon cumin
salt to taste
6 corn or flour tortillas,
warmed on griddle
4-6 cups fresh Enchilada Sauce, page 83

Sauté first four ingredients. Add corn, 3 cups of the cheddar, olives and cumin. Mix with a little Enchilada Sauce. Spread a little Enchilada Sauce on the bottom of a glass 9 x 13 inch casserole pan. Place about 1/2 cup filling into each tortilla and roll up, then place edge side down in pan. Cover with remaining sauce. Sprinkle with remaining cheddar cheese. Cover and place in refrigerator until ready to bake. This dish can be frozen at this point.

Bake at 350° for about 30 minutes. If the dish has been frozen, thaw completely before baking. Cool ten minutes before removing enchiladas from pan for serving with salad, beans and/or Spanish rice.

1 roasted chicken,
pulled into bite-sized pieces
1 bunch green onions, chopped
1 papaya, peeled and chopped
3 carrots, sliced thinly or julienned
1 cucumber, peeled,
seeded and sliced in small pieces
1 small jicama, peeled
and chopped into bite-sized pieces
Four flour tortillas,
cut into thin, 3 inch pieces
and fried according to recipe for
Chips on
page 82
cilantro to taste, chopped
(with whole leaves
left over for the top of the salad)

Toss all ingredients together in a bowl, then lightly toss with **Margarita's Cilantro Dressing**.

Margarita's Cilantro Dressing

1/2 cup cilantro
1/4 cup olive oil
1 Tablespoon lime juice
1 clove finely minced garlic
pinch of Mexican oregano
salt to taste

Combine and blend all ingredients in a blender or food processor.

Pasilla Pepper Rellenos
*Pasilla peppers are my favorite for Chili Rellenos –
perhaps because they are mild, full-flavored
and really easy to stuff.*

> 2 pounds large,
> roasted and peeled
> fresh Pasilla peppers
> 3-6 large cold eggs
> 1/4 cup flour
> 1 cup each of shredded cheese,
> shredded seasoned chicken
> or other filling of choice – be creative
> deep fryer
> or a large pan with 2 inches of oil
> pinch of salt
> paper towels for draining

Roast the peppers on a hot grill or in a broiler on high heat, turning occasionally until the skins are blackened and charred. Remove from the heat and let cool to room temperature. Peel skin from the cooled peppers, being careful to not tear the peppers while peeling.

Make a small slice into the side of the peppers, just big enough to get a spoon into, about 2-3 inches. Gently scrape the seeds and membrane out without tearing the peppers.

Carefully spoon the filling into the peppers. Even more carefully, coat stuffed peppers with flour. Set aside.

Beat 3-6 cold egg whites in a chilled bowl until they are stiff. Beat the yolks and slowly fold them in with a pinch of salt.

One at a time, hold the peppers by the stem and dip into the batter. Carefully place them into a pan with 1 1/2 inches of hot oil. Cook each side until batter is a crisp golden brown.

Remove peppers from the oil and drain on paper towels. Serve immediately with salsa of choice.

Tomatillo Sauce

3 pounds fresh tomatillos,
paper peeled away
and coarsely chopped
1 cup each, chopped: yellow onion,
carrots, celery
1 cup finely chopped almonds
2 cloves garlic
2 Tablespoons olive
or canola oil
1 can mild green chilies, diced
1-2 quarts chicken
or veggie stock*
1 teaspoon cumin
salt

Combine Tomatillos, onion, carrots, celery, almonds and garlic. Sauté
in oil until almonds are golden and vegetables soft. Add chilies. Blend
with hand held soup blender. Add stock and cumin and simmer about
30 minutes, until it thickens and is somewhat reduced. Salt to taste. Can
be frozen or held in refrigerator until ready to re-heat and serve. Can be
used in place of Enchilada Sauce.

HBD Book One – The Farm, pages 111, 114

Tortilla Soup

vegetable or corn oil
2 cups fresh or frozen corn,
thawed, patted dry
and pan-roasted in
1 Tablespoon butter
1 teaspoon ground cumin
1 medium yellow onion, chopped
3 carrots, chopped
3 stalks celery, chopped
3 cloves garlic, chopped
1 to 2 chipotle peppers
1 large can stewed tomatoes
1 small can tomato sauce
salt and pepper
3 cups chicken or veggie stock*
1 cup shredded Cheddar cheese
1/2 cup sour cream
3 cups tortilla chips, page 82,
cut into thin strips

Heat two tablespoons oil in a large soup pot. Add onions, carrots, celery, garlic and chipotle peppers. Cook vegetables 5 minutes. Add tomatoes, tomato sauce and 1/2 stock. Blend with hand-help soup blender. Add remaining stock and simmer. Add pan-roasted corn. Serve soup with shredded cheese and sour cream. Top with tortilla strips.

HBD Book One – The Farm, pages 111, 114

Stacked Chicken Enchiladas

9 x 13 inch glass baking dish

1 roasted chicken,
pulled into bite-sized pieces
1 yellow onion, chopped
3 carrots, chopped
3 stalks celery, chopped
1 clove garlic, diced
2 Tablespoons canola
or vegetable oil

3-4 cups cheddar
or Mexican blend cheese, grated
1 small can diced green chilies
3-4 cups Enchilada or Tomatillo Sauce,
pages 83 and 93
6 corn tortillas

Sauté onion, carrot, celery and garlic in oil at medium high temperature until soft and lightly caramelized. Blend with pulled chicken pieces, about 1 cup of sauce, 3 cups of cheese and chilies to taste. Pour and spread around a small amount of sauce into baking dish. Lay two corn tortillas down onto sauce to cover the bottom. Spread 1/2 of the filling over tortillas and repeat, ending with the third set of tortillas on the top.

Pour remaining sauce over to cover tortillas. Sprinkle with remaining cheese. At this point, the Stacked Enchiladas can be tightly covered and frozen for future use. If frozen, thaw before baking at 350° for about 40 minutes, or until cooked through and bubbling. Cut into square serving pieces.

Serve with rice, beans and/or salad and, of course, salsa of choice.

Tomatillo & Black Bean Tacos

2 Tablespoons canola oil
12 tomatillos, cut in bite-sized pieces
1/2 yellow onion, chopped
1 cup fresh or frozen corn (thawed and drained)
1 can black beans, rinsed and drained
1/2 small can diced green peppers (optional and to taste)

4-6 corn tortillas

Sauté and caramelize tomatillos, onion and corn in hot canola oil. Add drained black beans and heat through. Serve on warm corn tortillas with choice of salsa.

Sopaipillas
Also known as Indian Fry Bread, it has a sweetness to it.
Can be used in place of tortillas or eaten as a snack.

2 cups organic white flour
3/4 teaspoon salt
1 1/2 teaspoons baking powder
1 1/2 teaspoons sugar
1 Tablespoon butter
About 1 cup milk
canola oil for frying

Sift flour with salt, baking powder and sugar. Cut in the butter with pastry tool or fork. Add milk a little at a time to form a soft dough. Cover bowl and set aside for 30 minutes. On a lightly floured board, roll into small rounds, large rounds or triangles, depending on how they will be served. Heat oil and fry a few pieces at a time, turning once to puff evenly and fry until golden. Drain on paper towel. Serve plain with butter, dusted with powdered sugar or as a base for a Taco Salad. Makes about two-dozen small or one dozen large pieces.

Caramel Flan (Baked Custard)

6 small ramekins
or a small pie plate
shallow pan
for hot water bath

Preheat oven to 350°

2 cups milk
1 vanilla bean,
split lengthwise
6 Tablespoons sugar
6 eggs, beaten

1/3 cup sugar

Place the milk and the split vanilla bean into a saucepan and simmer for five minutes set aside to cool. Scrape insides of vanilla bean into the milk before mixing in the 6 Tablespoons sugar and beaten eggs.

While the milk is cooling, melt the 1/3 cup sugar – shake, don't stir. Once the sugar is melted, it will caramelize. At this point, pour it immediately into the ramekins or the pie plate. Protect your hand with hot pads and tilt to cover the bottom with the caramelized sugar. Do this quickly, as the sugar will begin to harden. Pour in the egg mixture. Set the pan with the hot water bath into the oven with just enough water to come up the sides of the chosen container for your custard, place the container(s) in the bath. Bake at 350° for approximately 25 minutes until just firm and a crack begins to form in the top.

Chill. As the Flan cools, the caramelized sugar will slightly dissolve. Before serving, loosen the edge of the custard, cover with a plate and invert. The Flan will slip right out, flowing with yummy caramel.

June, 1967
Dear T,

I met this guy named Gary Copperfield, the local hippie DJ, at the
Carmel Laundromat. I didn't know he was a hippie at the time. I didn't
even know what a hippie was until last week. I know I haven't just
dropped off that famous turnip truck full of bumpkins heading for the
west, but we were sheltered on the Farm.

Burned Turnips
By James Baker

When you are upset
And the baby's all wet
And the older children are yelling;
The turnips are burning,
The meat needs a turning
And the Jello just isn't jelling;

Or – the house is a mess
And you need a clean dress
And the bread man wants to collect –
You wish you could scream,
"It's all a bad dream!"
Does all of this sound quite correct?

It happens this way
And the experts will say
"Relax and give thoughts to your Blessings."
If you had them there,
You'd tell them just where
They could go with their sweet talk and guessings.

But the next day is shiny
And the kids are not whiny
Three cheers for a life full of fun!
Bring on any trouble –
In fact, make it double
You can do whate'er's to be done.

Oh, this is the life
Of a mother and wife
And often you find that's it's harried
But you wouldn't exchange it –
You never would change it,
You're really glad that you're married.

To T, continued

While loading three machines with his sheets, socks
and boxers, Gary was surreptitiously checking out
Gloria's pale blue seersucker suit, stockings, blue and
white spectator pumps, straw hat and white gloves
(honestly) - all juxtaposed against her amazing glossy
red lips. He quickly struck up a conversation. But,
really, how could you not strike up a conversation with
a babe dressed like that, gloves and all, doing her laundry?

Me? I was in jeans and a T-shirt, loading dryers with wet dishtowels,
and learning from a woman named Rosa how to fold fitted sheets into
themselves so they lay flat in the linen closet, while Gary and Gloria
discussed haute couture, politics and classical vs. pop music.

It was OK. The result was an invitation to the Monterey Pop Festival,
which Gloria politely declined. Little Glory, however, was up for the
adventure.

What a hoot! Gary introduced me to all these fringed and bangled folk
selling food, art and clothing; I heard Janis Joplin doing Ball 'n Chain
and was pretty much mesmerized (like any good bumpkin just off the
turnip truck) when Jimi Hendrix set fire to his guitar and bashed it on
the stage in a frenzy of fire and lust and song and, I don't know what,
something, powerful. I can still hear it like an echo in my head... wild
thing, you make my heart sing...

Gary and I munched hot **Crunchy Falafel Sandwiches** in brown paper
wrappings, nibbled **Deep Fried Artichoke Hearts** out of greasy wax
paper cones and drank paper cup after cup of Arnold Palmer's iced tea
and lemonade combo. I wandered around the Monterey Fairgrounds,
day and night, blitzed by colorful African Dashiki shirts and India-
Print dresses; wild hair braided with feathers and beads or shimmering
with gold dust; tattooed navels; wafting aromas from this Tibetan
incense or that sizzling pan; and... an intense pulsing base line running
through everything, like the in-sync heartbeat of a herd of wildebeests,
pounding all as one.

I helped a tall, white haired gentleman in overalls paint perfect and symmetrical peace symbols on the sides of his red VW Bus – having just then learned what a peace symbol was! I liked the idea of it. I watched four teenaged brothers kick a hacky-sack around a circle and let a young dreamy-eyed girl paint a psychedelic butterfly on my face.

psychedelic - newest word in my vocabulary.

I have arrived in California at the apex of the Summer of Love.

When Gloria's washing machine broke down, I never thought it would spark another adventure.

G

Crunchy Falafel

Middle East fast food. As a main dish, it is served as a sandwich, stuffed in pita bread with lettuce, tomatoes, and Tahini. Can be served as an appetizer, on a salad, or with hummus and Tahini. Falafel can also be formed into larger patties and served like a burger.

1 cup dried chickpeas
1 large onion, chopped
2 cloves of garlic, chopped
3 Tablespoons of fresh parsley, chopped
(I also like cilantro,
although I am not sure
it is traditional)
1 teaspoon coriander
1 teaspoon cumin
2 Tablespoons flour
salt
pepper
oil for frying

Soak chickpeas overnight in cold water. Drain and place in pot with fresh water, and bring to a boil. Allow to boil for 5 minutes and then simmer for about an hour. Drain and cool.

Combine chickpeas, garlic, onion, coriander, cumin, flour, salt and in a food processor. Blend until a soft paste forms. Form the mixture into small balls and flatten slightly. Fry in 2 inches of hot oil until golden brown (5-7 minutes). Serve hot.

To Gloria from James
Forever

You've been married for years
And you're up to your ears
In children and didies
And cookies

If you'd married the other guy
Backed by your mother, why
Now you'd be mixed up
with bookies.

But you still cook for me and
Wash socks and make tea
And still all the time
We play hooky.

Ah, you took that chance
For real-life romance
And what did it give to you?
Me!

Deep Fried Artichoke Hearts

2 eggs
1/2 cup milk
1 pound baby artichokes,
trimmed and quartered
1 1/2 cups seasoned
dry breadcrumbs
2 cups oil for frying,
or as needed
1/4 cup grated
Parmesan cheese
for topping

Heat oil in a heavy deep skillet. Whisk together eggs and milk. Place
seasoned breadcrumbs in a separate bowl. Dip artichoke hearts in
the egg mixture, then roll in breadcrumbs until they are fully covered.
Deep-fry for 2 to 3 minutes, until deep golden brown. Remove to paper
towels to drain excess oil. Sprinkle with Parmesan cheese before serving
(warm).

Tabouli Bulgur Wheat Salad

2/3 cup water
1/3 cup bulgur
1 Tablespoon salt
1 teaspoon ground cinnamon
3/4 cup fresh lemon juice
1/2 cup olive oil
1 3/4 pounds tomatoes, chopped
2 onions, finely chopped
2 bunches fresh parsley, chopped
1 bunch fresh mint, chopped

Bring the water to a boil in a small saucepan over high heat. Remove from the heat, stir in the bulgur, cover, and let stand 20 minutes. Spoon the bulgur into a mixing bowl, and add remaining ingredients. Gently stir, then refrigerate uncovered at least 1 hour until cold.

August, 1967

Dear T,

I have hunted down the recipe you asked me about to go with your
Mom's Mexican Dinner Party Theme. I love recipes with attached
legends. And the school library has a giant section on Mexico.

First of all, like "curry" in India (curry powder is a western invention),
"molé" simply means "sauce" – molé is Mexican Spanish, from Nahuatl.
We (gringos) generally think of molé as a chocolate dish but it doesn't
always have chocolate in it.

The story goes that the chocolate version was invented on the fly by
some poor nuns in Santa Rosa Convent (or maybe a monk named Fray
Pasqual, depending on the storyteller), in Puebla, Mexico, surprised by
a visit from the archbishop.

They dashed together a sauce of this, that and the other (spices,
veggies, chilies, nuts), threw in a hunk of chocolate just for kicks and
an ancient turkey they'd just dispatched for the occasion. It made
such an impression on the archbishop that it became the best-known
molé (sauce) in Mexico. But, all kinds of ingredients can go into a
molé – pumpkin, cinnamon, plantains, garlic, onions, miscellaneous
vegetables... whatever. This molé? Has chocolate! And peanut butter!

G

Here's the recipe:

Turkey Molé

12 Ancho chilies,
roasted, skinned,
stemmed and seeded
3 cups cooked turkey (not necessarily old),
pulled from the bones
or cut into small pieces
3 tomatoes,
roasted and peeled
1/4 cup canola oil
1 onion, peeled and sliced
3 cloves garlic
1 teaspoon cinnamon
1 Tablespoon Mexican oregano
1/4 cup peanut butter
1 clove garlic, minced
1/4 cup cornmeal masa
1 teaspoon cocoa powder
1/4 teaspoon thyme
1/4 teaspoon anise seeds
1/4 cup raisins,
soaked in hot stock to soften
salt and pepper to taste
4 cups chicken or turkey stock

Heat the oil in a large saucepan. Add in the onions and garlic and cook until translucent. In a food processor, add peanut butter, oregano, cinnamon, anise, thyme and garlic and blend with the tomatoes. Puree to make a smooth paste. Add in the onions and garlic and puree again. Finally, add Ancho chilis and purée once more. Add with stock to large pot and stir well.

Mix the cornmeal masa with a 1/4 cup of the chicken stock to blend. Mix this into the stock with cocoa powder, thyme and raisins and whisk until smooth. Simmer for 1 hour until thickened.

California Journal
January, 1968

I am sitting in my new apartment in Carmel, in the smallest living room on the planet. My sofa is the loveseat from Gloria's garage and the rest from the Thrift Shop in Monterey. The kitchen is the size of my closet, the stove has two burners. My mattress is still on the floor.

The other day, I went to a silk screening class with my "studio" paraphernalia all a-jumble in a brown paper bag. I was sorting through the bag trying to find stuff when I looked up to see this lovely woman sitting across from me pulling out her tools from a handmade, perfect fabric envelope-case thingy, with slots for every item - cutters here, pencils there... I, not too nicely, said, "God, you're organized!" She sort of peeped at me over the top of her glasses, which were perched on the end of her nose, paused and, in this Lauren Bacall voice said, "My dear... It makes life infinitely easier." Ha!

And, when I came home from that class, I found the newest tenant at my apartment building, Tracy, painting furniture in her front yard. She'd made curtains and painted her kitchen bright yellow. I asked, "Why are you going to so much trouble if you will only be here a year?" She pretty much gave me the same astonished look as the woman above, like I was this completely clueless idiot, and said, "Because I live here!" Ouch.

After two weeks, the mess in my room – OK, my whole apartment- is impressive. I pondered these two statements all evening while I picked up after myself. Messages from the gods, I think.

With a 30" x 40" piece of mat board and red and black markers, I have made a sign for my closet door, which is the first thing I see when I wake up in the morning. It states:

I hope this works, because I hate being a mess. My kitchen can't be a mess if there is going to be any room for vegetarian experiments.

Fruited Vegetable Sauce over Couscous

2 Tablespoons olive oil

1 onion, chopped
2 cloves garlic, minced
1 carrot, sliced
1 zucchini, sliced
1/2 teaspoon cinnamon
1/2 teaspoon salt
1/2 teaspoon cumin
1/4 teaspoon allspice
1 cup dry white wine
1/2 cup dried apricots, diced
1/2 cup dates, pitted and diced
2 cups cooked chickpeas
1 cup cilantro

Sauté the onions, carrots and garlic in olive oil. Add zucchini and continue to sauté until zucchini is softened. Add remaining ingredients except cilantro and simmer for ten minutes. Serve over couscous with cilantro sprinkled on top.

Couscous

1 1/2 cups couscous
2 1/2 cups water
salt
1/8 teaspoon turmeric

Place ingredients in a saucepan and simmer about twenty minutes. Set aside.

Veggie Burgers

3 cups water
2/3 cup barley
2/3 cup brown lentils
2/3 cup Basmati rice
1/4 cup vegetable oil
2 cups grated carrots
1 cup chopped celery
1/4 cup sunflower seeds
2 teaspoons dried crumbled thyme
1 teaspoon dried crumbled oregano
4 large eggs, beaten
7 Tablespoons flour

Bring water to boil. Add barley, rice and lentils. Cover and cook until tender – about 40 minutes. Transfer to large bowl and cool. Sauté vegetables in hot oil until tender – about 12 minutes. Add to grains and cool. Mix in seasoning and salt to taste. Stir in beaten eggs and flour. Form about 1/4 cup mixture each into patties. Heat oil in large skillet, add patties in batches and cook until golden, about five minutes each side.

Alice B. Toklas Brownies

*Although "Alice B. Toklas Brownies" is a household phrase, she was, by all accounts, clueless. My understanding is that while compiling interesting information for the book about her life with Gertrude Stein, she received the recipe for "******* Fudge" from one of her artsy Bohemian friends, and therefore claimed no personal knowledge of the subject.*

And the result was not brownies or fudge at all, but more of a fruit nugget, with an herbal addition.

A Monterey version from Gary Copperfield:

1/2 teaspoon
ground black pepper
1 teaspoon nutmeg
2 Tablespoons ground cinnamon
1 teaspoon ground coriander

A half-cup each: pitted dates,
dried figs, raisins,
shelled almonds
or other nuts, chopped
A handful of pulverized herbs
A cup of sugar dissolved in
2 Tablespoons warmed butter

Roll into balls about the size of a walnut.

According to Alice (or her friend):

"Two pieces are quite sufficient."

12 Individual Vegetable Pot Pies

For Filling:

2 Tablespoons butter

Cut the following into bite-sized pieces:
2 cups carrots
3 cups potatoes
6 stalks celery
2 cups broccoli florets

3 Tablespoons flour
3 cups vegetable stock
1 teaspoon tarragon
1 teaspoon oregano
1 teaspoon rosemary
salt and pepper to taste

1 package frozen peas, thawed
(or fresh, of course, but don't cook them)
1 package frozen corn, thawed (ditto)

Sauté fresh vegetables in butter until tender. Sprinkle with flour and blend in. Slowly add the vegetable stock, stirring constantly to keep from getting lumpy. Add herbs. Simmer for five minutes until thickened. Add peas and corn. Let cool completely.

4 cups white flour
1/2 teaspoon salt
2 sticks unsalted butter,
cut in pieces
1 cup cold water
or orange juice

Place flour, butter and salt in food processor and process until mealy. Slowly add cold juice or water through the top hole in the food processor until the dough comes away from the sides of the container and forms a ball. Use only enough juice or water to bind the dough together. When the ball of dough forms, stop processing. The less you process dough the better. Dust with flour and refrigerate about thirty minutes. This should make about 12 individual pies or one large pie.

Preheat oven to 350°

When ready to put the pies together, remove dough from fridge and cut into 12 equal pieces (for 12 pies). Roll out into circles and place in small pie tins with dough extended over the edges, which you will turn under and "flute" along the edges. Fill with cooled vegetable mixture. Sprinkle with **Savory Crumb Topping**. Place pies on a baking sheet covered with parchment and bake for about 35 minutes or until browned and bubbly.

Savory Crumb Topping

2 cups white flour
1 1/2 stick unsalted butter,
cut in pieces
1/2 teaspoon salt
2 Tablespoons dried parsley

Blend in food processor. Freeze leftover topping in Ziploc bag for later use.

Lemon Poppy-seed Cake

Back in the 50s, this cake might have been made with a yellow cake mix and warm Jello poured over the top. Ho boy.

6 Tablespoons milk
6 large eggs, separated
3 teaspoons vanilla
2 Tablespoons poppy seeds

3 cups sifted cake flour
juice of two lemons
and 2 Tablespoons lemon zest
6 Tablespoons powdered sugar
1 cup brown sugar
1 1/2 teaspoon baking powder
1/2 teaspoon salt

3 sticks unsalted butter,
softened

Preheat oven to 325°

Mix milk, egg yolks and vanilla. Sift together dry ingredients. Add butter and half of egg mixture to dry ingredients. Beat at high speed for one minute. Add rest of egg mixture and beat again. Beat egg whites until stiff and fold gently into cake mixture. Bake in well sprayed or oiled Bundt pan for 40 minutes or until slight cracks appear in the top. Let cake rest for about twenty minutes. Carefully remove from pan and place upside down on a serving plate.

Glaze with 1/2 cup sugar and 1/2 cup lemon juice, which you have brought to a boil before pouring over cake.

GORP – "good old raisins and peanuts." Or Trail Mix.

Trail Mix is simply a mix of things to eat on the trail. I've seen recipes
using Chex Mix and M&Ms, but I prefer more natural ingredients and
the combo I first discovered, in 1967 at the Monterey Pop Festival,
was simply a variety of nuts and seeds and dried fruit, maybe some
coconut. If adding chocolate or carob, remember they might melt in your
backpack!

Ideas:

raisins, currants,
cranberries, apricots, dates,
or other dried fruit
crystallized ginger
almonds, cashews,
macadamias, peanuts, pistachios
sunflower seeds,
toasted pumpkin seeds (pepitas)
coconut
chocolate chips,
yogurt covered raisins,
chocolate covered raisins,
carob nibs, cacao nibs,
coffee nibs

Great Granola
Fruit sugars only • low fat

2 cups organic rolled oats
1/4 cup sesame seeds
1/4 cup nuts, such as almonds,
walnuts or pine nuts
1/4 cup sunflower seeds
2 Tablespoons cinnamon
1 Tablespoon cardamom
1/2 teaspoon salt, optional
2 Tablespoons grated orange peel
1/2 cup apple or orange
juice concentrate, thawed
1/2 cup date pieces
1/2 cup raisins or currants
1/2 cup mixed dried fruit pieces
1/2 cup coconut, optional

Pre-heat oven to 325°

In a large mixing bowl, combine the oats, seeds, nuts, spices and orange peel. Add the juice concentrate and mix well with large wooden spoon. Spread mixture on parchment covered baking sheets - bake for about 45 minutes or until lightly toasted and dry. Cool before adding fruits and optional coconut. Omit the coconut for less fat.

1970

August, 1970
Dear T,

Bringing you up-to-date on

My Life at The Gingerbread Farm...

Sorry it's taken so long... I disappear into relationships, sometimes, I
know.

Albert is light-years older than I (16 years) – British, quite dashing
– when we met in Carmel on a street corner, he was wearing a bush
jacket with an ascot and this rather jaunty hat with the brim turned up
on one side.

I didn't invite you to the wedding because we got married by a Justice
of the Peace during our lunch hour. Really. Even Gloria didn't know
until later. Guess I am not destined for a formal wedding with, like,
guests and all that this lifetime.

Our marriage, in food terms, is a kind of face-off between British
comfort (meat and two veg) and what Albert calls my "bushes and
weeds" (vegetarian). We face-off over most everything: straight rows
verses meandering garden paths; how to distribute chicken feed (in a
container? or tossed?); or whether to call our liquid garden fertilizer
that we make in giant tubs Chicken Poop Soup or Chicken Manure Tea,
just for starters.

Well, he's interesting. He likes Billy - they drive go-carts together and
fly radio-controlled airplanes and sail on Albert's boat on Monterey Bay
and Albert taught Billy how to ride his new bike. We found this little
Farmette together and it all just seemed to work out.

It's not a Farm farm, but an acre on the river with this great little
house, barn and chicken coop and plenty of room for a garden. I loved
my little apartment, but we have space here. And a kitchen bigger than
a flour bin. And Billy has a good daddy.

G

Carrot Cake

2 cups flour
1 1/4 teaspoon baking powder
1 teaspoon baking soda
1 teaspoon cinnamon
1/2 teaspoon salt
2 cups brown sugar
1 1/4 cup canola oil
4 eggs, beaten
3 cups carrots, grated

Preheat oven to 350°

Sift together dry ingredients. Cream together sugar and canola oil, about two minutes. Slowly add eggs. Blend with dry ingredients. Add grated carrots and blend in.

Spray a Bundt pan or baking dish. Pour batter into pan. Bake at 350° for approximately 40 minutes. When cooled, drizzle with a mixture of 2 tablespoons orange juice and about 1/2 cup powdered sugar, or enough to make a thick frosting. This cake is also fabulous without frosting, or with cream cheese.

Changes

Life on the Farm was all that it should be
I didn't or couldn't know what I would be
I married early and gave birth to a child
I didn't go crazy or act very wild
But suddenly life has grown very tall
I am an adult, with baby and all

I've gone from one Farm to another, it seems
I've changed my ideas and altered my dreams
My son has a home, a father, a garden
For those disappointed, I just ask your pardon
Cause life has a way of changing your plans
And you do what you can with what's in your hands

GSB

Making Bread

Labor Day, 1970
Dear T,

Bread is my thing. Gloria's Gloria has nothing on me - she may have her cookies for holiday baskets – I want to master bread.

I am writing to you from a Zen Mountain Center, deep inside the Las Padres Forest east of Carmel. I have just finished reading the Tassajara Bread Book like a romance novel. Mr. Brown's kitchen: spotless copper pots and pans, a candle burning on the chopping block to quiet the mind, dish-washers (all young, earnest men with slight figures and sweet Jesus beards), smiling and humming while sloshing in the dishwater. The rows and rows of fresh loaves waft the most beautiful aromas – onion and poppy seed and sesame, oat and barley and wheat, all crusty and perfect.

Lunch here is a smorgasbord of natural, vegetarian treats – fresh bread, soups, luscious salads, Baked Eggs, **Mushroom Veggie Loaf with Mushroom Sauce**. If you pack your own lunch for a hike (the Narrows is this kind of natural singing waterway on the hill above the monastery where you can swim in the buff if you want) your choices fill a whole room: 10 kinds of bread, spreads, every kind of filling and veggie; nut butters and aiolis; jellies and jams; goat and cow and sheep cheeses; sprouts and lettuce and thinly sliced cabbage, deep red mountain-grown tomatoes, spicy salsas and chutneys; sprinkles of this and shakers of that. Trail Mix. The garden here is amazing – one monk's job is watering hours on end. Like painting the Golden Gate Bridge - he starts at one end and by the time he's done, it's time to begin all over again.

How are the wedding plans coming? I'll be there with bells on!!!

G

Mushroom Veggie Loaf with Mushroom Sauce

2 Tablespoons butter or canola oil
1 onion, diced
1 1/2 cups mushrooms, chopped
2 cloves garlic, diced
1 Tablespoon each dried thyme,
savory & marjoram
1/2 teaspoon dried sage, crumbled
1 1/2 cups cooked brown rice
1 1/2 cups pecans, chopped
½ cup cashews, chopped
4 eggs, beaten
1 cup cottage cheese
¾ cup grated Cheddar cheese
¼ cup mixed fresh herbs
(parsley, oregano, thyme)

Preheat oven to 350° - this recipe makes one loaf

Heat butter or oil in a large skillet. Sauté onion on medium high until lightly caramelized. Add mushroom, garlic and dried herbs. Sauté until mushrooms are browned and the liquid is evaporated.

Place cooked vegetables in a large bowl. Add all remaining ingredients and toss well. No salt is necessary, since the cheeses are salty enough!

Line the bottom and sides of a 9 inch bread loaf pan with parchment, leaving about 3 inches to overhang the sides. Coat the parchment with Baking spray. Fold mixture into the pan, rapping the pan on the counter to release any bubbles. Fold parchment over the top.

Bake at 350° for one hour or until firm. Cool about fifteen minutes. Unfold parchment and turn your loaf onto a platter. Serve with mushroom sauce and steamed vegetables.

Mushroom Sauce

1 onion, sliced
2 pounds mushrooms, sliced
1 clove garlic, minced
2 cups **Dark Veggie Stock***
2 Tablespoons cornstarch
1 teaspoon soy sauce

Sauté onions, garlic and mushrooms on medium high until lightly browned and the liquid evaporates. Add 1 1/2 cups vegetable stock. In remaining stock, mix 2 Tablespoons cornstarch and add to sauce. Add Soy Sauce or season to taste. Bring to a boil to thicken. Serve immediately or re-heat.

Above the stove in my Gingerbread Farm kitchen, glass gallon jars filled with grains, seeds, nuts and berries (all the accompaniments to bushes and weeds) are crammed together on redwood shelves that Albert built; a hand-crank grain grinder has miraculously attached itself to the end of the counter; a juicer and all its parts fill up a corner. My windowsill is full of sunflower sprouts.

My friend and neighbor, Carletta Smith, joined me on my sunny porch one morning last week while I was wrapped up in a tale of how to make a Swedish Tea Ring. She plunged along with me into the baker's world. For the next five days, we baked, the summit of which will be putting our holiday baskets together.

Our first Tea Rings were a bit lopsided - our two kids raced through the front door and out the back, oblivious of our trays in front of the fire. A regular stampede of little booted feet through rising rings of dough. We baked them anyway.

Phase 1
1 cup lukewarm water
1 Tablespoon active dry yeast
2 Tablespoons brown sugar
or molasses
1/3 cup dry (powdered) milk
1 egg
1 1/2 cups unbleached organic flour,
whole wheat or white

Phase 2
3 Tablespoons melted butter
or vegetable oil
1 teaspoon salt
2 1/2 cups flour

One of the main things I learned about baking bread, thanks to Mr. Brown, is that phase 1 is about rising, phase 2 adds the salt. If the salt is added in phase 1, it will have a negative, or slowing down affect on the yeast's growth. The sugar feeds the yeast and allows it to fully develop.

In **Phase 1**, the warm water is placed in a warm bowl and sprinkled with the active dry yeast. The sweetener of choice is added, along with the dry milk, which gives a lighter texture, and in the case of sweet bread like cinnamon rolls, an egg. This is then beaten with a spoon, while adding in the first phase of flour. Beat 100 times. Let the "sponge" rise for about an hour before you begin phase 2.

Phase 2 adds the salt, oil or butter and the remaining flour. When enough flour is folded in to begin pulling the dough away from the sides of the pan and the dough no longer feels wet to the touch, it is time to turn it out onto a floured board and begin the hand-over-hand kneading process. This usually takes 10-15 minutes, until the dough is smooth and bounces back to your gentle touch.

Place the dough in an oiled bowl and let rise for about an hour. Punch it down and let rise again.

Phase 3
raisins
cinnamon
melted butter
egg wash (one egg beaten with one Tablespoon water)

For Cinnamon Rolls, roll out the risen dough to an approximate 12' x 14' rectangle, about 1/4 inch thick. Brush with melted butter and sprinkle with raisins and cinnamon. Roll it up, cut into sections and place flat onto a sheet covered with parchment. Let rise about 20 minutes. Brush with egg wash and bake at 375° for approximately 20 minutes.

Before cooling, you can drizzle the warm rolls with a mixture of one cup powdered sugar and two or three Tablespoons orange juice.

Swedish Tea Rings
To make a Swedish Tea Ring,
follow above instructions for Cinnamon Rolls through Phase 2.

For filling, simmer until thickened (while dough is rising):

> 1 cup chopped date pieces
> and raisins
> 1/2 teaspoon cinnamon
> 1 Tablespoon lemon juice
> 1/4 cup brown sugar
> 1/8 teaspoon salt

Cool completely and spread on the 12' x 14' roll. Roll up as for cinnamon rolls, shape into a circle and place on the parchment covered baking sheet. Cut 1-inch slits into the dough with scissors and twist the roll to expose part of each slice. Bake as above. Before cooling, you can drizzle the warm rolls with a mixture of powdered sugar and orange juice and dot with candied fruit.

1/2 cup hot water or apple juice
1/2 cup mixed dark
and light raisins
1/2 cup chopped dates
1 1/2 Tablespoon butter
3/4 teaspoon soda
3/4 cup plus
2 Tablespoons flour
1/2 cup brown sugar
1 egg
1/2 teaspoon vanilla
1/4 cup chopped nuts

Heat oven to 350°. Pour hot water or apple juice over raisins, dates, butter and soda. Let stand. Sift flour. Mix flour, sugar and salt well; add fruit mixture and remaining ingredients. Beat well; pour into greased and floured 1 pound coffee can (This is so 50s! I don't even buy coffee in cans anymore. But a loaf pan will do just as well). Bake 60 to 70 minutes.

Bananas Foster
JR's Favorite dessert

1/4 cup (1/2 stick) butter
1 cup brown sugar
1/2 teaspoon cinnamon
1/4 cup banana liqueur
4 bananas, cut in half
lengthwise, then halved
1/4 cup dark rum
4 scoops vanilla ice cream

Combine the butter, sugar, and cinnamon in a skillet. Cook over low heat, stirring, until the sugar dissolves. Stir in the banana liqueur, and then place the bananas in the pan. Carefully add the rum when the banana sections soften and begin to brown. Cook the sauce until the rum is hot. Tip the pan slightly to ignite the rum. When the flames subside, lift the bananas out of the pan and place four pieces over each portion of ice cream. Generously spoon the warm sauce over the top of the ice cream and serve immediately.

2 cups peanut or almond butter,
smooth or crunchy
1 cup butter, softened
5 cups confectioners' sugar
2 (12-ounce) packages of chocolate chips
(white
and/or semisweet)

In a medium-size bowl, combine the nut butter and butter and stir with a wooden spoon, until evenly blended. Add the confectioners' sugar and stir until the mixture has the consistency of dough. Roll into 1-inch balls and place on parchment paper on a baking sheet. Put the baking sheet in the freezer until the peanut butter balls are solid enough to pick up with a toothpick, about 30 minutes.

Melt the chocolate chips in a microwave or in a double boiler.

Insert a toothpick into each peanut butter ball and dip it into the melted chocolate. Set the chocolate-coated balls on a baking sheet lined with waxed paper. Remove the toothpicks. Immediately place a chocolate or peanut butter chip over each toothpick hole. Cool in the refrigerator until the chocolate has hardened, about 5 minutes. Makes about 100.

Date* Nuggets

1 cup date pieces*
1/2 cup almonds
or pine nuts
1/2 cup coconut
1/4 cup sunflower seeds
2 teaspoons maple syrup
1/4 cup toasted sesame seeds,
for rolling

Combine the first five ingredients in a food processor and whir until the nuts are crushed and the whole thing forms a kind of sticky dough. Scoop out about 1 teaspoon at a time, forming into balls and roll in toasted sesame seeds. Refrigerate for about an hour. These keep well in the freezer.

*Or cranberries, or raisins, or any dried fruit

Thanksgiving, 1970

Dear T,

My family will never let me forget this. Remember the pastry queens,
Gloria and Aunt Eleanor? They could whip up a flaky crust in a
matter of minutes, with their bare hands! On the Farm, Gloria washed
her hands and dipped them into her bowl of flour and chopped cold
butter. She rubbed through it with her fingers, creating the perfect
mealy texture that is required for the crust to flake. Remember this?
Remember Aunt Verna teaching me about Puff Pastry, not so long ago?

OK. So, I got it into my head this year, I plead temporary insanity, that
fresh milled whole wheat flour, vegetable oil and honey would be a
better and healthier approach to pie making, so sure was I that whole,
natural ingredients were the way to go. In fact, I was so sure about this
that I told Gloria not to bring a pumpkin pie– I WOULD DO IT MYSELF!
The Gingerbread Farm way.

The result was something akin to the foundation of our house. Martin
stabbed the whole pie in the center with his fork, lifted it in the air, and
carried it around the room like a solid silver
trophy for the world's worst pie. Remind me to
never do this again.

Thank you for the picture of us at your
wedding. You look really beautiful and
happy. Hope you come to visit me soon. I have
collected lots of cool recipes for you, per your
request (including Gloria's pie crust – not
mine!).

G

California Journal
January 1972

I first thought of British food as gray, overcooked vegetables, fish & chips, pickled herring and kippers, and dishes with cute names: Cullen Skink, Cockie Leekie, Finnan Haddie, Tweed Kettle. Marrying a Brit has opened my eyes at The Gingerbread Farm. Great Cornish Pasties are side by side with salads and alfalfa sprouts.

Cornish Pasties

A pasty is a turnover, filled with savory meat and or potatoes (Tiddy Oggies), using leftovers, cheese, gravy, veggies, whatever. In the nineteenth century pasties were the lunch of choice, easily slipped into pockets. Make the filling first and let it cool completely while making the Shortcrust Pastry.

Filling

1 Tablespoon oil
1 onion, chopped
1 carrot, chopped
2 stalks celery, chopped
1 potato, chopped
1 pound ground meat
(beef, lamb or chicken)
1/2 cup stock
blended with 1 Tablespoon flour
salt and pepper to taste
herbs of choice

Sauté the vegetables in hot oil until tender, about ten minutes. Add the ground meat and continue cooking until meat is done. Add stock and flour and herbs of choice and bring to a boil to thicken. Salt and pepper to taste. Set aside to cool.

2 1/4 cups flour
1/4 teaspoon salt
3 ounces unsalted butter
4 ounces lard
(found in most markets –
but you can just use
7 Tablespoons of butter instead)
1 egg yolk
3 Tablespoons cold water
egg wash,
made with a little milk
to brush on the tops

Place all ingredients in the food processor and whirl around until it barely holds together to form a soft dough. Knead the dough gently, wrap in plastic and chill for about 30 minutes.

Pre-heat the oven to 400°. Roll the pastry to a thickness of about 1/4 inch. Cut into 6-inch rounds (for four large) or 3-inch rounds (for eight small). Lay the rounds on a baking sheet covered with parchment and place a mound of filling on one side. Brush the edges of the pastry with egg wash. Fold the pastry over the filling to form a half circle. Pinch edges together. Make little steam escape slits in the tops. Brush with remaining egg wash. Bake for 30 minutes or until golden. Serve warm with gravy or room temperature for the lunch box.

Welsh Rabbit

2 1/2 cups grated Cheddar cheese
(real Cheddar –
not grated rat cheese
in a bag –
it doesn't melt)
1 Tablespoon butter
1/2 cup beer or ale
2 teaspoons Coleman's dry mustard
or Grey Poupon
salt and pepper to taste
toasted English muffins
or bread

Melt the cheese with the butter and ale in a saucepan. Add the mustard and salt and pepper. Arrange the toast or muffins on a baking sheet covered with parchment. Pour the cheese mixture over the toast and broil until the cheese is browned and bubbling. Slip servings onto plates with a spatula.

Toad in the Hole

8 sausages
1 Tablespoon oil

Yorkshire Pudding Batter

6 eggs
Pinch salt
2 1/4 cups milk
3 1/2 cups flour
4 Tablespoon melted butter
1 Tablespoon maple syrup

This batter should be made the night before serving, or at least in the morning, to give it a chance to cure.

Blend the eggs and salt in the food processor for about 1 minute. Add 1/2 the milk and 1/2 the flour and blend. Add the second half of each and blend again. Add melted butter and maple syrup. Blend well. Pour into a pitcher and refrigerate. (One mistake most people make is preparing the batter just before baking).

When ready to bake, cook the sausages in the hot oil in a frying pan. Set aside. Drain the dripping into a pre-heated baking dish to coat. Distribute the sausages evenly in the baking dish. Stir the batter to blend in the curing bubbles and pour over the sausages. Bake at 350° for about 40 minutes, or until the Yorkshire Pudding is puffy and golden. Pierce the Yorkshire Pudding with a skewer to release steam (so it won't collapse).

Remember:
Yorkshire Pudding/Popover Batter

• Make the batter a day ahead and keep chilled, to allow it to "cure."

• Pre-heat the oven with the baking pan in it before you spray it or coat it with oil.

• Add the cold batter and put it back in the oven immediately.

• When removing from oven, pierce popovers or pudding with a skewer to release steam, so they won't collapse.

Really. This works. Flawless.

Cornish Game Hens

Cornish Game Hens aren't the least bit British,
having been invented by crossbreeding
in Connecticut in the 1950s.
They're good, though.

4 little birds, thawed completely
1 cup apple juice mixed with
1/2 dry white wine
Small mixture of herbs,
such as thyme,
oregano
and rosemary,
rubbed between your fingers
8 small red potatoes, cut in half
6 carrots,
cut in large pieces
1 white onion
cut in large pieces or
12 pearl onions
3 Tablespoon flour

In a sprayed baking dish, place the birds and the juice/wine mixture and herbs and cover with foil. Roast at 350° for 45 minutes, basting occasionally. Remove foil, add the side veggies, which you have tossed in the flour, and continue to roast, basting often. When the birds are brown and the vegetables are tender, your dinner is ready! (This should take another 25 minutes or so.) The flour will have created a bit of gravy to serve over your one-dish meal.

Shortbread

2 cups butter
1 cup packed brown sugar
4 1/2 cups all-purpose flour

Preheat oven to 325°

Cream together butter and brown sugar. Add 3 to 3 3/4 cups flour. Mix well. Sprinkle board with the remaining flour. Knead for 5 minutes, adding enough flour to form a soft dough. Roll to 1/2 inch thickness. Cut into 3x1 inch strips. Prick with fork and place on parchment covered baking sheets.

Bake at 325° for 20 to 25 minutes.

1971

Sunday, Valentine's Day, 1971

Dear T,

I am writing to you from my perch on the porch (with my handy
companion, the red portable typewriter – it even has sand in it from the
beach) watching everyone else walking up the trail toward the lake,
with fishing poles and trout bait (salmon eggs, balls of raw bread dough
and mini-marshmallows).

We were invited (with five other couples, their various offspring and
any canine companions) to a 14,000 square foot house with twelve
bedrooms and 20 beds on a beautiful sunny 2,000-acre ranch on the
Russian River, near Occidental.

Remember Halton? She was the one who cut your bangs about 1/4 inch
long when we were playing with scissors in Gloria's sewing room on
the Farm. We were about 8. She's the daughter of Gloria's friend, Betty.
Anyway, this ranch was available to Halton's boyfriend, and here we
are.

The instructions were to bring three bags of groceries. That's all. She
sent us a map.

So, there were thirty bags of groceries, and guess who ended up in
charge of the kitchen? Yep!

It's been fun, really, making stuff out of whatever is in those bags
– everything from Rice Krispies Treats to Bisquick pancakes and
bacon, **Turkey Meatloaf** and grilled cheese sandwiches with pickles
and onions (thanks to your dad - his original recipe) and a fabulous
Rosemary Roasted Chicken. If I see trout in a few hours, we'll have
it with mashed potatoes and vegetables for dinner. Otherwise, we are
down to mashed potatoes and vegetables for dinner. Ha Ha. Good thing
we're leaving tomorrow.

My Bags:

English muffins, bacon, lots of salad stuff, olive oil, rice wine vinegar, mustard, maple syrup, vegetables, fruit, spices and herbs, eggs from our chickens, oatmeal, pizza sauce, pita bread, flour, yeast, baking soda and baking powder, brown sugar, yogurt, coffee, wine

From others:

Rice, veggies, pickles, alfalfa sprouts, beer, bread, coconut milk, Granny Smith apples, cantaloupes, watermelon, peaches, nectarines, orange juice, apple juice, milk, potatoes, eggplant, ground beef, sliced turkey, whole chickens, cereal, tea, coffee, peanut brittle, pineapple, cottage cheese, Bisquick, marshmallows, graham crackers, chocolate, and other things I can't even remember already.

We've eaten well, with everyone pitching in to chop, grate, mix, blend, serve and wash up.

We have hiked, played cards and Charades, gathered in a group around the fire with our guitars and flutes and tambourines, watching our small children build blanket forts in the giant living room, older children build real forts outside out of fallen logs and branches, swum in the river. But mostly, we sit on various porches and swings, talking, eating and drinking lemonade, hot chocolate, beer, wine and coffee.

Love G

P.S. Later... Trout fishing was successful, but the biggest fish was about as large as my pinky. Lots of them, though.

Turkey Meatloaf

2 onions, chopped
3 carrots, chopped
3 stalks celery, chopped
2 Tablespoons olive oil

1/2 teaspoon salt
Dash pepper
2 Tablespoons dried thyme
1 Tablespoon dried tarragon
1 Tablespoon fennel seeds

4 pounds ground dark turkey
2 eggs
1 cup breadcrumbs

Sauté onions, carrots and celery (mirapoix) in hot oil until softened. Add spices and let cool.

Mix cooled mirapoix with ground turkey, eggs and breadcrumbs. Form into two loaves and place on baking sheet covered with parchment. Roast about 1 1/2 hours at 350°. Let stand about 15 minutes before serving.

Rosemary Roasted Chicken
with Roasted Root Vegetables

2 organic chickens, in single serving pieces
olive oil
salt and pepper
3 Tablespoons fresh crumbled rosemary
1 cup apple juice
4 large Yukon Gold potatoes, cut in quarters
4 carrots, cut in large pieces
2 parsnips, cut in large pieces
10 pearl onions, peeled
4 stalks celery, cut in large pieces

Oil or spray the bottom of a large roasting pan. Arrange pieces of chicken in pan. Sprinkle with salt, pepper and crumbled rosemary. Cover pan with foil and poach chicken in apple juice for 45 minutes at 350°.

Remove foil cover. Place vegetables around chicken pieces, baste with liquid in roasting pan. Return to oven for approximately 40 minutes, basting regularly. Serve when chicken is browned and tender and vegetables are golden and cooked through.

Thank You

February, 1971

Dearest Glory,

It strikes me as so terribly funny that I should have a house party and be writing you a thank you note! As much as I appreciated your cooking all weekend, more than that, I dig how you dig it! Everyone raved about you and your cooking. We dig you a bunch and you really helped pull things together.

So, thanks not only for the fabulous cooking – which really was so beautiful, I can't believe it – but thanks for helping everyone feel comfortable and warm and good about the weekend.

If we join a commune, will you join up as chief cook?

Much love,

Halton

1972

September, 1972
Dear T - This is Fall at

The Gingerbread Farm
Apricot Orchard

10 Apricot Trees = many bushels of apricots
= Jam, Fruit Leather, Pies & Bread

Our Friend Sam always arrives just in time to help. For an old guy (50, at least) he's agile on the ladder.

Sam lives on his 40 acres in two 12 x 12 tents perched on the decks we found together, the three of us, on our walk of the property the day his real estate deal was signed. It was a boon, finding those decks in the middle of practically nowhere. No one knows who built them or when. They were just... there. He'll live in his tents on his decks until his new home is built.

Sam's giant paintings hang in the oak trees. His "shower" is a black plastic bag of water hanging on a branch, warming in the sun. His kitchen: two outdoor shelves, a hand built counter and a camp stove nestled under an awning.

He sleeps on our sofa bed when the rain gets him down. Or when he has a cold. Or when he's just plain tired of camping out: no matter how cool or Bohemian it sounds, it has its limitations.

Recipes for all things apricot enclosed.

G

Apricot Jam

8 cups chopped apricots
1/4 cup lemon juice
6 cups sugar
5 pint canning jars or
10 half-pints with lids.

Sterilize jars by boiling for 10 minutes in a hot water canner.

Combine all ingredients in a large stockpot. Bring to boil over medium-high heat, stirring occasionally until the sugar dissolves.

Once mixture reaches a good boil, simmer for 30 minutes, stirring often to prevent sticking. Remove from heat and fill jars, leaving 1/4 space at the top.

Wipe rims of jars clean and put lids in place.

Process in boiling water canner for 10 minutes.

2 cups blended apricots
1 Tablespoon lemon juice
2 Tablespoons honey

Cut apricots in half and remove pits. Blend smooth in a food processor or blender. Add honey and lemon juice and blend again. For more intense fruit flavor, cook the apricots for 30 minutes, then blend and let cool before the next step.

Prepare a baking sheet with plastic wrap covering the bottom. Pour the mix onto the plastic wrap and smooth with a spatula. It should be about 1/8 inch thick.

The trays can be placed outside in the sun covered with a screen or cheesecloth (not touching the mixture) or placed in a 140° oven overnight. When dry, roll up in its plastic wrap and store in refrigerator or freezer.

Apricot Pie

4 cups sliced fresh apricots
1 cup sugar
1/3 cup flour
pinch ground nutmeg
1 Tablespoon lemon juice
1 pastry recipe for double-crust 9-inch pie
milk
additional sugar

In a large bowl, toss apricots, sugar, flour and nutmeg. Sprinkle with lemon juice; mix well. Line a 9-in. pie plate with bottom crust; add filling. Roll out remaining pastry. Place over filling; seal and flute edges. Brush with milk and sprinkle with sugar. Cover edges of pastry loosely with foil. Bake at 375° for 45 minutes or until golden brown.

Apricot Bread

1 cup apricots, chopped
1 cup sugar
2 Tablespoons butter softened
1 egg
3/4 cup orange juice
2 cups all-purpose flour
2 teaspoons baking powder
1/4 teaspoon baking soda
1 teaspoon salt

In a mixing bowl, cream the sugar, butter and egg. Stir in orange juice. Combine flour, baking powder, baking soda and salt; stir into creamed mixture just until combined. Add apricots to batter. Pour into a greased loaf pan. Bake at 350° for approximately 50 minutes or until a crack appears along the top. Cool a few minutes in pan before removing to a wire rack.

I love it. Elsa and Hans Brandenburg live on a little farmette across the road on the sweetest slope of land that can't be more than three acres. Big enough, though, to have 50 chickens, six ducks, 12 milk cows, six bee hives, fruit trees, blackberries and the most luscious terraced garden in the Valley. Our membership in Elsa's private little co-op, we call it "Owning Half a Cow," allows us a gallon of fresh milk and a box of vegetables per week.

I drive up their driveway on Saturdays, and park in the circular part in front of their barn, painted a soft blue. To the left of the barn is a small "outbuilding," the same blue; like a milk house, only so much more. In the frosty fridge is a glass gallon jar of milk with our name on the lid. The cream on top of the milk is two inches thick. On the floor is our box of veggies. Next to the fridge is a table full of goodies: honey, eggs, fruit jams, beautiful cakes; more vegetables in baskets and trays. I leave Elsa a note about my purchase and milk payment, leave my check or cash in an envelope, take change from the little dish. I love this.

If we arrive at the right time, we get to see or participate in some cool farm thing, like spinning honey from honeycombs in their giant extractor, or collecting berries and fruit.

FREE
Lunch
NEXT
DOOR

Carmel Journal
March 1972

Hm. You can take the girl off the Farm, but...

- I look at my self and see some of the old me, the girl who was born for this: Chickens. Eggs. Turkeys. (Well they're dead, but more on that later).

Big ol' garden, a pony named Indian for Billy, fresh milk from Elsa, a kitchen full of grains and grinders and a window full of herbs. Two cats in the yard, and all that. I am right at home and kind of happy.

Billy's certainly happy. He found the Free Lunch Next Door sign and told me that I always had to have it pointing toward my kitchen. And I promised him I would. I posted it on the fridge for now. It is pointed toward the sink.

I pause for a moment to ponder the two dead turkeys: the general belief is that they died of stupidity. In January, Albert put the turkey chicks in the greenhouse for warmth and isolation from the chickens - to acclimate them to their new surroundings. Several weeks later, we moved them into the chicken run, for company - birds of a feather and all that. Two weeks ago, the turkeys were dead, of dehydration and starvation, since we never could convince them of the change in dining venue. They kept going back to the greenhouse and banging their heads on the glass door to get in. We kept picking them up and taking them back to the chicken run and poking their beaks into the feed trough, like one would train a dog or cat. Forget turkeys. My turkey training was a complete failure- but perhaps turkey training is an oxymoron.

No fresh turkey for the Holidays after all. They would have been pets by then, anyway, as neither Albert nor I or any of our peace loving friends would actually be able to do away with Tom and Joe (Thomasina and Josephina? We didn't know for sure).

191

Hard Boiled Eggs

Place eggs in single layer in saucepan. Cover with at least one inch of cold water over tops of shells. Cover pot with lid and bring to a boil over medium heat. As soon as the water comes to a full boil, remove from heat and let stand.

For large soft-cooked eggs - let stand in hot water 1 to 4 minutes.

For large hard-cooked eggs - let stand in hot water 15 to 17 minutes.

When ready to your taste, drain off hot water and cover with cold water and ice. This will make them easier to peel.

Coddled Eggs

Butter (or non-stick spray) the inside of an egg coddler and its metal lid. Break 1 or 2 eggs into the cup, and season to taste with pepper and salt.

Other ingredients can be added to the egg coddler before cooking (such as grated cheese, chopped herbs, chopped bacon). Adding a dash of cream is rich and filling.

Gently, lightly and loosely, screw on the lid
Stand the egg coddler in a pan of boiling water halfway up the porcelain coddler. Don't submerge it.

Simmer for 5 to 8 1/2 minutes, depending on the size of your coddler and the size of your eggs (see chart). Cold eggs take longer.

Small Coddler
1 large egg - 5 1/2 minutes
1 medium egg - 5 minutes

Large Coddler
2 large eggs - 8 1/2 minutes
2 medium eggs - 6 1/2 minutes

By lifting the ring, remove the egg coddler and set on a towel, or trivet (not on a cold surface. Twist the lid by the sides of the ring to loosen it.

Serve at the table in the coddler (set on a saucer with a folded napkin, perhaps) with toast or cheese sandwiches or potatoes.

Shirred or Baked Eggs

1/4 teaspoon softened butter
2 teaspoons heavy cream
2 eggs
salt and pepper to taste
1 teaspoon minced fresh chives
1 teaspoon grated Parmesan cheese or Swiss cheese

Preheat oven to 325°. Rub the inside of a 6 ounce ramekin with butter or non-stick spray. Pour cream into the ramekin and gently, so the yolks don't break, crack the eggs on top of the cream. Wiggle the yolks toward the center. Sprinkle with salt, pepper, chives, and Parmesan cheese.

Bake in preheated oven 12 to 15 minutes, until the whites of the eggs have set and the yolks are still soft. Allow to "set" outside the oven for 2 to 3 minutes before serving.

Poached Eggs

fresh eggs
1 to 2 teaspoons seasoned rice vinegar
shallow saucepan with cover
glass measuring cup
slotted spoon

Bring water in a saucepan to almost boiling. Add vinegar to help the egg whites to congeal more easily. (If you have an egg poacher, you can avoid all this below).

Working with the eggs one by one, crack an egg into the glass cup, then place the cup near the surface of the hot water and gently slither the egg into the water. Wiggle the egg whites closer to their yolks to encourage the egg whites to hold together.

Cover and turn off the heat. Let stand for 4 minutes, until the egg whites are cooked.

Gently lift eggs out of the pan with a slotted spoon.
Or, put all eggs into the egg poacher cups, place on the boiling water. Remove from heat and cover... and all the rest.

Breakfast Burrito

Oh, Breakfast Burritos! The morning cook's friend! Scramble whatever you want (eggs, tofu, with milk, without) with whatever you want (veggies, cheese, mushrooms, more cheese, chopped cooked meats) and wrap in a warm tortilla! With or without salsa. The best!

Eggs Benedict

Eggs Benedict are traditionally an English Muffin, halved and toasted, with a piece of breakfast meat (ham, Canadian bacon) topped with a poached egg and Hollandaise Sauce, said to be created by either, 1) Mr. Whoever Benedict, who thought a "hooker of Hollandaise" might be just the thing to cure his hangover or, 2) Mrs. Benedict, who was bored with breakfast.

There are as many variations of Eggs Benedict as stars in the flag (fresh salmon, poached salmon, smoked salmon, arugula, bacon, spinach, mushroom.....) but the most important thing is a good **Hollandaise Sauce**.

Hollandaise Sauce

4 egg yolks
1 Tablespoon freshly squeezed
lemon juice
1/2 cup unsalted butter,
melted (1 stick)
pinch cayenne
pinch salt

Whisk the egg yolks and lemon juice together in a stainless steel bowl until the mixture is thickened and doubled in volume. Place the bowl over a saucepan (or in a double boiler) containing simmering water - the water should not touch the bottom of the bowl. Continue to whisk. Be careful not to let the eggs get too hot or they will scramble. Slowly drizzle in the melted butter and continue to whisk until the sauce is thickened and doubled in volume. Remove from heat, whisk in cayenne and salt. Cover and place in a warm spot until ready to use for the eggs benedict. If the sauce gets too thick, whisk in a few drops of warm water before serving.

Huevos Rancheros

olive oil
1/2 medium onion, chopped
1 15-ounce can whole fire-roasted tomatoes,
or 1 -2 large fresh vine-ripened tomatoes
1/2 6-ounce can diced green Anaheim chilies
Chipotle chili powder
Enchilada Sauce, page 83
ground cumin to taste
4 corn tortillas
butter
4 fresh eggs
2 Tablespoons fresh cilantro,
chopped (optional)
grated cheese

For the Sauce: in a large skillet, soften the onions in olive oil on medium heat. Add the canned tomatoes with their juice. Break up the tomatoes with a fork. For fresh tomatoes, chop and add to onions. Note that fresh tomatoes will take longer to cook than pre-cooked, canned tomatoes. Add chopped green chilies and chili to taste, with chipotle chili powder, Enchilada sauce, regular chili powder, and/or cumin. Bring to a simmer, reduce heat to low, and let simmer for 10 minutes. Add salt to taste if needed.

For tortillas: Heat the oven to 150°, place plates in the oven to keep warm. One by one (or more if your pan is big enough) heat the tortillas in the pan in hot oil, a minute or two on each side, until they are heated through, softened, and pockets of air bubble up inside of them. Stack in a warm towel while you continue cooking the rest of the tortillas and the eggs.

Fry the eggs in the same skillet, add two teaspoons butter to the pan for 4 eggs. Crack 4 eggs into the hot skillet and cook for 3 to 4 minutes.

Spoon sauce onto a warm plate; add a tortilla, a fried egg, more sauce, sprinkled with grated cheese and cilantro. Two per hungry person.

Avgolemono
(Greek Chicken/Lemon Soup)

1 small free-range chicken
2 quarts water
2 Tablespoons olive oil
1 onion, finely diced
2 bay leaves
1 leek, cleaned and quartered
1 carrot, peeled and quartered
2/3 cup Arborio rice
2 large eggs
1/2 cup fresh lemon juice
1 Tablespoon salt
1 teaspoon ground pepper

Place the chicken in a large pot with 2 quarts cold water, enough to cover the chicken. Bring to a boil and reduce heat to low, skimming when necessary. Simmer for about 1 hour.

Heat 2 tablespoons of olive oil in a saucepan and add the onions. Sauté the onions until they are translucent. Set aside.

Remove chicken from stock. Let cool and "pull" (not cut) the meat from the bones. Set aside. Add the onion, bay leaves, leek, and carrot to the stock and simmer for 1 hour. Remove carrot and leek from the stock and add the rice. Bring to a boil and then simmer 30 minutes. Add the chicken back into the stock.

Beat the eggs and lemon juice together in a small bowl. Pour 2 cups of stock slowly into the bowl of egg and lemon, whisking continuously. Once all the stock is incorporated, add the mixture into the pot of chicken soup and stir to blend well throughout. Salt and pepper to taste. Serve hot.

Fresh and Delicious Frittata

smoked or sautéed salmon, in bits
mini Roma tomatoes
Cooked carrots, sliced thinly
green onions, chopped
roasted potatoes, sliced thinly
Cheddar and Parmesan cheese
handful of chopped Italian parsley

Place the sliced salmon and the other ingredients gently into a sprayed glass 13 x 9 inch baking dish.

Pour over it a well-blended mixture of:
8 eggs
½ cup half & half

Sprinkle with Parmesan. Bake in 325° preheated oven for about 40 minutes, until slightly firm – but remember, it will keep cooking for a bit when you remove it from the oven, so don't overcook it.

Crème Brulée

1 quart heavy cream
1 vanilla bean,
split and scraped
1 cup sugar, divided
6 large egg yolks
2 quarts hot water

Preheat oven to 325°

Place the cream, vanilla bean and pulp into a saucepan over medium-high heat and bring to a boil. Remove from heat, cover and set aside for 15 minutes. Remove the vanilla bean and discard.

In a medium bowl, whisk together 1/2 cup sugar and egg yolks until lightened in color. Add cream a little at a time, stirring continuously. Pour liquid into 6 8-ounce ramekins. Place ramekins into a roasting pan. Pour enough hot water into pan to come partway up the sides of the ramekins. Bake until the Crème Brulée is set, but not firm, about 40 to 45 minutes. Remove ramekins from roasting pan and refrigerate for about 2 hours or up to 3 days.

Remove from the refrigerator for at least 30 minutes prior to browning the sugar on top. Divide remaining 1/2 cup sugar equally among the 6 dishes and spread evenly on top. Slide under a broiler or use a torch to melt the sugar and form a crispy top. Set aside for at least 5 minutes before serving. Serve with a dollop of whipped cream with a sprig of mint, or a coffee bean, or a thin cookie.

1976

California Journal
Fall 1976
Dinner in the Neighborhood

Black E Brown, poet, artist, host, drifted from room to room, carrying round glass bowls of green salad crowned with orange and yellow nasturtiums; silver platters with egg rolls bathing in plum sauce. Big crockery pots exploded with giant red and orange zinnias. The carpeted floor was strewn with cushy, colorful, oversized pillows: stripes and floral prints and solid colors. Chimes jingled and bamboo clacked in the wind. Soft music whispered in the background. In the fireplace and outside in a shallow pit, burning embers sparked and crackled and snapped. The light was low and warm. Our faces had soft, ethereal glows.

Egg Rolls

4 tablespoons vegetable oil
1-inch grated fresh ginger
2 cloves garlic, finely chopped
2 scallions, thinly sliced
1 carrot, cut into thin julienne strips
1 cup Napa cabbage, shredded
1/4 cup chicken stock
2 tablespoons soy sauce
1 Tablespoon sugar
2 Tablespoons sesame oil
20-24 wonton wrappers covered loosely
with a damp paper towel to prevent drying
10 shrimps,
grilled or sautéed and minced
or 1 cup cooked lamb
or pork
or chicken
or beef

In a wok or skillet, stir-fry ginger and garlic in 2 tablespoons of oil about 30 seconds. Add scallions and carrots and stir-fry over high heat for 2 minutes. Add the Napa cabbage and cook for five minutes, until the vegetables are soft. Add sesame oil, cool for at least 15 minutes, and strain.

In a saucepan, combine stock, soy sauce, and sugar. Bring to a boil and simmer 5 minutes, stirring occasionally. Add vegetables. Fold in the minced shrimp or meat (or use vegetable stock and no added meat for vegetarian egg rolls).

Place one wonton wrapper with one corner closest to you. Place a teaspoon of the filling in the center of the wrapper. Roll the corner closest to you over the filling and brush the top corner with water. Fold in the wonton sides and continue rolling up until it is closed. Press to seal, set aside, and continue with remaining ingredients.

In a skillet set over moderately high heat, heat the remaining oil and sauté the egg rolls until golden brown on all sides, turning several times. Serve when cool enough to eat, with dipping sauce.

Plum Sauce

1 cup plum jam
1 Tablespoon vinegar
1 teaspoon onion powder
1/4 teaspoon ginger powder
1/4 teaspoon allspice
1/2 clove garlic, crushed
salt and pepper to taste
1/3 - 1/2 cup of water
(depending on thickness of jam)

Mix the ingredients together well. Bring to a boil on low heat. Cool the sauce and store in a jar in the refrigerator. Use within a few days.

Dipping Sauce

1/3 cup soy sauce
1/3 cup rice wine vinegar
1 Tablespoon honey or sugar
2 Tablespoons dark sesame oil
pinch of red pepper flakes

Combine all ingredients.

It's your movie
You are
The writer, director & star.
If you're not
You become an extra
In someone else's plot.

Black E Brown

Seasons Change

Perfume fills the air
Lilacs bloom everywhere
Every hue
Pale lavender to blue
Bursting at the seams
The Gingerbread Farm
Is celebrating
After winter waiting
Spring will be here
Then summer is near
Sun and fun
And then too soon
The leaves leave
And then the pumpkin patch
Another year too swift to catch
And then it's two
And another winter moon
I'm ready
Soon

BEB

October 1976

Dear Black E,

Thank you so much for the poem in honor of The Gingerbread Farm Pumpkin Patch - and the recipe for your Pumpkin Soup. I hear it's legendary (a little bird with initials BEB told me the other night at my dinner table).

I enclose the recipe for my equally famous Mushroom Barley Soup. If you make it with morels in the spring (John Orman will dig some up for you – he has a nose for morels), it is beyond famous and legendary, but thrilling and delicious and worthy of tasting in your dreams.

Glory

PS: Thanks for your wonderful dinner, too, by the way. Your parties are like being inside a Monet painting.

THANK YOU!

Pumpkin Soup

4 Tablespoons unsalted butter
2 medium yellow onions, chopped
2 teaspoons minced garlic
1/8 to 1/4 teaspoon crushed red pepper
1/2 teaspoon ground ginger
1/2 teaspoon ground coriander
1/4 teaspoon cinnamon
1/4 teaspoon ground cumin
5 cups puréed cooked pumpkin
8 cups chicken or vegetable stock
1 cup coconut milk
1/2 cup brown sugar
salt to taste

Melt butter in a 4-quart soup pot over medium-high heat. Add onions and garlic and cook until softened, about 5 minutes. Add spices and cook for a minute.

Add puréed pumpkin and stock; blend well. Bring to a boil and reduce heat, simmer for 10 to 15 minutes.

Using a hand held soup blender, blend soup until smooth and creamy. (this step may be omitted for a chunkier soup). Add brown sugar and coconut milk.

Serve in individual bowls. Top with a dollop of sour cream blended with milk – if you use straight sour cream, it just might sink to the bottom. Sprinkle with nutmeg or toasted pumpkin seeds or **Fried Parsley.**

Fried Parsley

4 cups Italian parsley, washed and dried
1 teaspoon cornstarch
salt

Heat 1 inch of vegetable oil in a saucepan over medium-high heat. Toss parsley with cornstarch. Fry in batches until crisp, about 30 seconds. Drain on paper towels and sprinkle with salt.

Mushroom Barley Soup

5 cups water
1 cup pearl barley
1/2 teaspoon dried thyme, crumbled
1/2 teaspoon dried tarragon, crumbled
1/3 cup minced fresh Italian parsley
salt and pepper to taste

3 cloves garlic, chopped
1/4 cup olive oil
3 medium onions, chopped
2 stalks celery, chopped
8 carrots, chopped
2 pounds white mushrooms, sliced thin
1 pound morels or chanterelles, sliced
1 Tablespoon soy sauce
1/2 cup sherry
5 cups chicken stock

Put water, barley, and dried herbs in a pot and simmer 1 hour.
In another large soup pot, cook garlic, onions, celery and carrots, in
oil over moderate heat, stirring, until golden. Add mushrooms and soy
sauce and sauté over moderately high heat, stirring, until the liquid of
the mushrooms is evaporated. Add sherry and simmer until evaporated.
Add stock and bring to simmer. Add cooked barley and simmer for 25
minutes.

Sprinkle with parsley. Drizzle with sherry before serving.

The Fondue Party
Fondue. Invented by the French in the 20s.
No, no, Swiss peasants in the 1600s.
No no, in New York City in 1950... well, whatever.

Cheese for starters...

1/2 pound imported Swiss cheese, shredded
1/2 pound Gruyere cheese, shredded
2 Tablespoons cornstarch
1 garlic clove, peeled
1 cup dry white wine
1 Tablespoon lemon juice
1 Tablespoon sherry
1/2 teaspoon dry mustard
pinch nutmeg
bread chunks, apples
or blanched vegetables for dipping

Toss the cheeses with cornstarch and set aside. Rub the inside of the fondue pot with the garlic and discard.

Place the fondue pot over medium heat; add wine and lemon juice and simmer. Gradually stir cheese into the simmering wine/lemon mixture. Once cheese is melted and smooth, stir in sherry, mustard and nutmeg. Place pot over its little flame.

Arrange an assortment of bite-sized dipping items on trays around fondue pot. Spear with fondue forks or wooden skewers. Dip, Drip and Eat.

Meat Fondue can be created several ways – in hot oil or in broth (which resembles the Mongolian Fire Pot or Japanese Shabu Shabu). The hot oil method is messier, a fire hazard in most dining rooms and not as healthy. Herewith is a Beef Broth Fondue. Use chicken, lamb or pork, in their related broths, for advanced fondue making.

Pour a good quality beef stock (preferably one which you have made yourself) into your fondue pot and bring to a simmer.

Roll a small piece of thinly sliced beef onto a fondue fork and cook for a few seconds or minutes, for rare, medium or well done. Add blanched vegetable pieces, if desired.

Chocolate Fondue for Dessert

1 pound bittersweet chocolate, chopped
2 cups heavy cream

Dipping pieces (such as bananas, strawberries, or other fresh fruit, dried fruit, small cookies, pound cake)

Combine chocolate and cream in the top of a double boiler over a pan of simmering water. Stir occasionally until chocolate is melted and mixture is smooth. Pour into heated Fondue Pot and serve with accompaniments.

Throw in a salad somewhere, and Voila-la!

Last night, we were ensconced on the sofa watching Monty Python's Flying Circus.

Gloria called, having a fit. Where are you?, she almost screamed.

Well, uhm, we are right here, on the sofa, watching....

I don't care what you're watching! You're supposed to be here!

What?

The Spencers, remember? They are expected for dessert any minute!

Mom. That's tomorrow night.

No it's not - it's tonight, Monday.

Mom. Gloria. The invitation was for Tuesday.

Well, this Grand Marnier Soufflé is about to come out of the oven, so you'd better high-tail it over here and pretend it's Tuesday!

Dutifully, off we high-tailed it to Gloria's. Good thing they live only four miles away.

Tonight, the real Tuesday, with the Spencers, we'll be having a Trifle. Gloria's taking no chances. And, besides, she can use the rest of that Crème Anglaise.

Grand Marnier Soufflé

6 Tablespoons unsalted butter
plus additional for buttering ramekins
1 cup sugar
plus additional for coating ramekins
1/4 cup plus 2 Tablespoons all-purpose flour
1 cup whole milk
7 large egg yolks
1/4 teaspoon vanilla
1/8 teaspoon orange oil*
2 Tablespoons Grand Marnier
8 large egg whites

Preheat oven to 400°

Generously butter eight 1 cup ramekins and coat with sugar, knocking out excess.

In a heavy 2 quart saucepan melt butter over moderately low heat and whisk in flour. Cook roux, whisking, 3 minutes. Slowly add milk and cook over moderate heat, whisking, until mixture is very thick and pulls away from sides of pan. Transfer mixture to a bowl and cool 5 minutes. In a large bowl whisk together yolks, vanilla, oil, and a pinch salt, and whisk in milk mixture and Grand Marnier, whisking until smooth. Cool.

In a large bowl with an electric mixer beat whites until they hold soft peaks. Beat in 1 cup sugar, a little at a time, and beat until it just holds stiff peaks. Fold one-fourth egg whites into yolk mixture to lighten and then thoroughly fold in remaining whites with a rubber spatula.

Spoon batter into ramekins just to rim and arrange in a large baking pan. Add hot water to reach halfway up sides of ramekins and bake soufflés in middle of oven 20 minutes, or until puffed and tops are golden.

Remove pan from oven and transfer ramekins to dessert plates.

Serve soufflés immediately with:

Crème Anglaise

1/2 cup whole milk
1/2 cup whipping cream
1 2-inch piece vanilla bean, split

3 large egg yolks
3 Tablespoons sugar

Combine milk and cream in heavy saucepan. Scrape in seeds from vanilla bean; add bean. Bring milk mixture to simmer. Remove from heat and remove bean.

Whisk egg yolks and sugar in medium bowl to blend. Gradually whisk hot milk mixture into yolk mixture. Return custard to saucepan. Stir over low heat until custard thickens and leaves a coating on the back of the spoon, about 5 minutes (do not boil). Cover and chill. (Can be made 1 day ahead.)

English Trifle

1 pound cake or sponge cake
1/3 cup sweet sherry or rum
1/2 cup raspberry jam
3 cups mixed berries
(sliced strawberries, raspberries, blueberries)
Other fruit, such as bananas or kiwi, sliced

For Custard (Or use Crème Anglaise)

8 egg yolks
1 1/4 cups sugar
1 teaspoon vanilla extract
2 cups whole milk
1/2 pint whipping cream
2 Tablespoons powdered sugar
strawberries, for garnish

Heat the milk in saucepan over medium low heat. Beat the eggs with the sugar and vanilla in a double boiler until it forms a ribbon. Slowly pour the hot milk into the eggs, beating all the time. Place the mixture in a heavy saucepan and stir over low heat until the custard coats the back of a spoon, 10 to 15 minutes. Don't boil. Cool completely.

Slice cake into one-inch pieces. Spread with jam. Cut into I inch cubes and layer half on the bottom of a glass trifle bowl, or any straight-sided glass bowl. Sprinkle cake with sherry or rum to soak. Dot with half the cut fruit, then half the cooled custard.

Repeat. Refrigerate, covered, at least 4 hours. Whip cream and spread over the trifle. Garnish with strawberries.

Large quantities of inexpensive food (I learned this from the Lady of Maples nuns!) that can be served on paper plates with plastic forks and knives (not from the nuns) for the myriad Bohemian flower children who drop by at dinner time at Glory's (also not from the nuns).

The Harper boys (Mark, Silver, Chad and Brett) live down the road, and they never arrive empty-handed. They were the boys tossing the hackysack at the Fairgrounds at Monterey Pop. They were darling then, more darling now. Albert put them to work - for some reason, they like to get bossed around by a strong male figure.

Together we've created the Fast Food Bars at The Gingerbread Farm: cheap, satisfying, and lots of it. Silver works at the Village Corner; Mark and Chad at a produce company; Brett likes to eat.

The Baked Potato Bar

Baked potatoes, halved and wrapped in foil

Toppings:
Butter
Sour cream
Cooked ground meat
Cheeses (Parmesan,
Cheddar, Swiss, Brie,
Gorgonzola)
Sprouts
Lettuce
Mashed avocado
Cottage cheese
Crumbled bacon
Caramelized onions
Green onions
Grated carrots
Roasted garlic
Grilled or sautéed chopped vegetables
(zucchini, peppers, onions)
Thimbles of sherry
Soy sauce

Taco Bar

Corn "taco shells"
Soft flour tortillas (warmed and in foil)

Fillings:
Cooked ground beef (cumin, garlic, chili powder)
Cooked sirloin steak slices
Roasted chicken or turkey (with or without sauce)
Pulled pork
Grilled shrimp
Grilled or seared fish (tuna, salmon, halibut, tilapia)
Black or refried beans
Caramelized or grilled vegetables
Shredded lettuce
Alfalfa sprouts
Grated or crumbled cheeses (Cheddar, Feta, Gorgonzola)
Chopped tomatoes
Chopped papayas
Guacamolé or sliced avocados
Jalapeño peppers
Sautéed tomatillos
Cilantro
Limes
Salsas

Gazpacho

Gazpacho

1 large can tomato juice
1 medium green bell pepper, minced
1 cucumber, peeled and minced
2 small canned green chilies, minced
1 Tablespoon Worcestershire Sauce
1/2 teaspoon garlic, minced
1 Tablespoon olive oil
1 Tablespoon chives, chopped
2-4 drops hot pepper sauce
salt and pepper to taste
one lemon, wedged

Combine everything except lemon and chill.
Serve with lemon wedges.

Several kinds of cooked pasta, kept warm in chafing dishes
Olive oil
Marinara sauce
Cream sauce
Alfredo sauce
Meatballs
Sausages (chicken or pork)
Roasted lamb
Cooked ground meat with Italian seasonings
Roasted chicken or turkey
Cooked sirloin strips
Grilled shrimp
Prosciutto
Grilled or roasted vegetables
Fresh arugula
Fresh Mozzarella
Shaved and/or shredded Parmesan and/or Romano
Basil pesto
Roasted garlic
Heirloom tomatoes
Anchovies
Raisins
Toasted pine nuts
Lemon

Caesar salad
Fresh green salad

Crusty loaves of bread

1977

August, 1977
Dear T,

I have just returned from my first official excursion as Camp Cook
on a weekend Trail Ride in the Las Padres National Forest. I met this
guy named Charles "Chuck" Waggoner, who is a gourmet chef with
a knowledge of the trail. I had made a fancy cake (in the shape of a
swimming pool with a shark swimming in the middle and a reclining
babe in a pool-side lounge chair) for a mutual friend's birthday pool
party and Chuck saw it - and hired me – my first cooking gig - for
money! Even before he tasted the cake! The money wasn't all that
great, but I didn't care. I was on a horse, in the woods, cooking, hiking
and hanging out by the fire. He even trusted my fire skills, which says a
lot, coming from a him.

Chuck has introduced me to the stinkiest cheeses, for which one must
develop a "nose," just like wine... or morels... he says. He brought the
cheeses. Phewy! We went shopping for the rest. He grilled the meats
and I made the accompaniments – various sauces for grilled meats,
potatoes and corn roasted in the fire-pit, eggs and bacon and oatmeal
for breakfast. Coffee served at first light in the guests' (8) tents.

I brought some of my **Preserved Lemons**! It was so much fun. Who
cares that I made about 17 cents an hour? We rode for about two hours
to a campsite in a clearing, with a fire-pit, picnic tables and little nooks
and crannies among the trees for little private sleep spaces and tent
sites. We schlepped the food in saddlebags – nothing that would spoil
in three days time. Chuck took the guests out for day rides (some went
hiking), I mostly stayed around the camp to keep the home (camp)-
fires burning and make stuff to eat.

I am also beginning to learn about wine (also thanks to Chuck). No
more Mateus for me! I am going to develop my nose for cheese and
wine!

G

Preserved Lemons
Moroccan, Russian, Indian, African...
who knows who made these up.
Ibn Battuta, considered one of the greatest travelers
of all time, ate preserved lemons in Somalia in 1325!

Meyer lemons
(enough to fill your jar)
salt
spices
(see below)
lemon juice

Slice the washed lemons lengthwise in quarters or slivers. Place in large mixing bowl. Have clean glass jars available. Toss lemons in Kosher or sea salt, using about one Tablespoon per lemon. Toss in several cinnamon sticks, or break them up so you have some for each jar, sprinkle with cumin seeds, peppercorns and a bay leaf or two. Toss well to distribute all spices.

Fill clean glass jars with lemon mixture.

Pour in lemon juice to cover all lemons.

Seal the jars in a hot water bath (water at a simmer) for 10 minutes. Not totally necessary if the lemons are refrigerated, but be safe.

Every few days for three weeks, turn jar(s) upside down and then right side up. Keep refrigerated.

Use on vegetable or meat dishes, as salad topping, in sandwiches. Use as part of a Gremolata (lemon, parsley, fresh garlic).

Pickled Grapes

1/2 cup vinegar
(white wine for green grapes,
red wine for red grapes)
1/2 cup water
1 bunch fresh tarragon or 1 Tablespoon dried
4-5 crushed coriander seeds
1/2 teaspoon crushed cumin seeds
1 crumbled bay leaf
1 clove garlic, crushed
1 cup seedless grapes

Combine first seven ingredients. Toss with grapes. Place in glass or plastic container. Cover and refrigerate 24 hours. Can be doubled, tripled, quadrupled...

Serve with grilled or roasted meats.

1 cup mashed avocado
1 whole canned Chipotle chili
1 1/2 Tablespoon juice of fresh lime
2 teaspoons white wine vinegar
1/2 cup plain yogurt
1 1/2 teaspoons toasted
and coarsely ground cumin seeds
1 teaspoon kosher salt
1/4 cup olive oil
1/2 cup cilantro

Purée all ingredients except cilantro in food processor. Add cilantro and pulse until it is coarsely chopped. Serve sauce at room temperature with grilled fish or chicken. Makes about two cups.

Papaya Poppy-seed Cream

1/2 papaya, peeled and seeds removed
1 clove garlic, chopped
2 teaspoons fresh ginger root, peeled and chopped
2 teaspoons mustard
1 teaspoon honey
1 1/2 Tablespoon raspberry vinegar
1/4 cup salad oil (hazelnut, walnut...)
1 teaspoon poppy-seeds

In food processor, blend papaya, garlic, ginger, salt, mustard, honey and vinegar. Continue to blend while pouring the oil through the top hole, until smooth and creamy. Stir in poppy-seeds. Serve at room temperature with grilled fish or chicken.

1 whole garlic head, topped
2 Tablespoons olive oil

2 cloves garlic, peeled and chopped
3/4 cup peanut or vegetable oil
2 ounces dried Ancho chilies
1/2 cup chicken broth
3 Tablespoons balsamic vinegar
2 Tablespoons brown sugar
2 teaspoons toasted and ground cumin seeds
1 1/2 teaspoons kosher salt
pepper
pinch of ground cloves

Pre-heat oven to 425°

Slice top off of whole garlic. Place on foil on baking sheet and drizzle with oil. Roast for about 25 minutes, until cloves are tender and browned. Set aside. Place Ancho chilies in pan of water and simmer until tender, about ten minutes. Remove from heat and let stand for an additional ten minutes. Drain and place in ice to loosen skins. Scrape flesh from skins into bowl.

Squeeze roasted garlic from husks and place in food processor with all other ingredients. Blend until smooth. Serve at room temperature with grilled meats, chicken or vegetable.

Corn Cakes
Great as a side dish or entrée

1 cup corn kernels
(either fresh or frozen)
1/2 cup grated carrots
1/2 onion, chopped

2 Tablespoons butter
salt and pepper

2 eggs, beaten
1 cup breadcrumbs

vegetable oil for frying

Sauté corn, carrots and onions in butter until slightly caramelized, about five minutes. Set aside to cool. In a bowl mix eggs and breadcrumbs. Add sautéed vegetables and mix well. Form into patties or croquettes. Fry in oil until golden, turning to fry all sides. Serve with Salsa or Warm Tomato Chutney.

Tomato Chutney

six large Roma tomatoes, quartered
1/4 yellow onion, chopped
1 Tablespoon cumin seeds
2 teaspoons brown mustard seeds
2 Tablespoons olive oil
2 Tablespoons Balsamic vinegar
2 Tablespoons brown sugar
salt and pepper to taste

Sauté tomatoes and onion in hot olive oil, with the cumin and mustard seeds. Cook until seeds pop and onions and tomatoes are softened. Add vinegar and brown sugar and cook until the moisture is absorbed, about five minutes. Serve warm or room temperature.

Tofu Cakes

1/2 cup grated carrots
1/2 onion, chopped

2 Tablespoons butter
salt and pepper

1 cup crumbled firm tofu
2 eggs, beaten
1 cup breadcrumbs

vegetable oil for frying

Sauté carrots and onions in butter until slightly caramelized, about five minutes. Mix with tofu, eggs and breadcrumbs. Form into patties or croquettes. Fry in oil until golden, turning to fry all sides.

1978

Fall, 1978
Dear T,

I have arrived! I'm in a cookbook! It is called **Cows and Poets** and has recipes by artists, writers, etc. in Carmel. Chuck Waggoner recommended me!

I am so completely jazzed to be part of this! I am sending you this copy so you can see how completely cool this is. My recipe is the **Mexican Soufflé** I made up for brunch the day I was asked to be in the book. I wonder what I would have come up with had I thought about it for more than two minutes.

Sam's contribution to the cookbook was "How To Eat an Apple," full of philosophical meanderings about the cosmos one finds in a fruit.
G

Mexican Soufflé

1 Tablespoon softened butter
1/2 cup shredded good quality Cheddar cheese

1/2 cup butter
1/3 cup flour
1 teaspoon salt
dash of pepper
1 teaspoon dry mustard
1 1/2 cups warm milk
1 cup shredded good quality Cheddar cheese
1 can chopped green chilies
2 cups fresh corn, roasted
   in a small amount of butter in a pan until caramelized
1 cup soft breadcrumbs
6 slices cooked bacon, crumbled
1 onion, chopped and sautéed
6 eggs, separated

With softened butter, butter a 2-quart soufflé dish and coat with 1/2
cup cheese. Melt remaining butter and blend in flour, to form a roux and
add salt, dry mustard and pepper. Over low heat, gradually add warmed
milk, stirring until thickened. Add 1 cup shredded cheddar, green chilies,
roasted corn, breadcrumbs, bacon, and sautéed onion. Remove from heat
and blend in egg yolks, one at a time. Set aside until completely cooled.

Fold in stiffly beaten egg whites. Gently pour mixture into soufflé dish.
Bake at 350° for approximately 50 minutes, or until golden. Serves 6-8.

California Journal
November, 1978

Dinner at the Carver's tonight. Met Emma. Had my first taste of Caviar Pie.

I thinking meeting a new girlfriend is better than falling in love. One hardly ever falls out of love with a good girlfriend.

Caviar Pie

3/4 cup minced sweet red onion
6 hard cooked eggs
1/4 teaspoon salt
1/2 teaspoon pepper
3 Tablespoons mayonnaise
8 ounces cream cheese
2/3 cup sour cream
1/4 teaspoon hot sauce
2 ounce jar black lumpfish caviar
2 ounce jar red lumpfish caviar

Place minced onion on a paper towel to absorb moisture.
Grease a 10" spring-form pan with a little mayonnaise. Mash eggs with
salt, pepper and mayonnaise. Spread into the bottom of pan. Spread
onions
on top of egg salad. Mix cream cheese and sour cream together until
smooth. Mix in hot sauce. Spread smoothly over the onions.

Recipe can be prepared up to this point the day before and refrigerated.
Place spring-form on a paper towel on a plate in refrigerator to absorb
liquid as sour cream separates.
Just before serving, carefully rinse caviars in separate bowls of water,
strain, and spread on towels to drain. Run a knife around the edge of the
spring form pan to loosen and remove the ring.

With caviar and perhaps some chopped green onion, create a design
on the top of the "pie," in the shape of a star or Christmas tree. Use
toothpicks to arrange caviar.

Serve with crackers or crostini.

Steamed Clams with Chorizo

1 medium onion, chopped
1 yellow bell pepper, chopped
1 garlic clove, minced
1/2 teaspoon cumin seeds
1/4 teaspoon salt
2 Tablespoons olive oil
3/4 cup dry white wine
2 pounds littleneck clams (2 inches wide), scrubbed
1/4 pound dried Spanish chorizo links, diced
2 Tablespoons fresh cilantro

Cook onion, garlic, cumin, and salt in oil in a 6-quart heavy pot over moderate heat, stirring occasionally, until vegetables are softened, 7 to 9 minutes. Stir in wine and bring to a boil.

Add clams and chorizo, then boil, covered, until clams open, 7 to 8 minutes, discarding any clams that do not open. Toss in cilantro and serve.

Serve with crusty bread or over linguine or rice.

Glory's Snap Pea Salad

3 cups fresh sugar snap peas, "stringed" and thinly bias cut
6 radishes, thinly shaved
½ cup fresh basil, thinly sliced (chiffonade*)
¼ cup Chêvre (goat cheese)
1 cup cherry tomatoes, cut in half
¼ cup toasted pine nuts
dash red wine vinegar
Splash olive oil
salt and pepper to taste

Combine all ingredients in a bowl and toss.

** Honey Baby Darlin' Book One – The Farm*

243

California Journal
Christmas 1978

I have decided to forgo baked goods and breads for my holiday baskets. It's a Truffles year.

And I have worked out the new version of Uncle Jon's favorite dessert – Baked Rum Fruit. I just can't bring myself to use canned cling peaches anymore…

50s version:
1 can cling peach halves
1 can pineapple chunks
1 can dark sweet pitted cherries
1 can apricot halves, reserve liquid
1 1/3 cup light cream
1 cup brown sugar
1 pint sour cream

1978 version:
2 cups fresh peaches, halved
1 cup dried pineapple, cut in pieces
2 cups dark sweet pitted cherries
1 1/2 cup pomegranate juice
1/3 cup light cream
1 cup brown sugar
1 pint sour cream

Preheat oven to 350°

Combine fruit and liquid in shallow three-quart baking dish. Sprinkle
with brown sugar and pour 1 cup rum over the fruit. Bake for 1 1/2
hours, uncovered, stirring once. Serve warm with sour cream.

German Chocolate Cheesecake

1 package German Baker's chocolate
1/3 cup milk
2 Tablespoons sugar
1 package cream cheese, softened
1 cup whipped cream
1 package graham crackers
½ stick melted butter

Heat chocolate and 2 Tablespoons of milk over medium heat. Stir until melted. Beat sugar into cream cheese, add remaining milk and chocolate mixture and beat until smooth. Fold whipped cream into chocolate mixture.

Blend together graham crackers and melted butter in food processor. Press into pie tin. Pour filling into crust. Freeze about four hours.

Garnish with whipped cream and raspberries or lemon twist.

Chocolate Truffles

1 cup heavy cream
10 ounces semi or bittersweet chocolate, chopped
5 Tablespoons unsalted butter
scant 1/4 cup Grand Marnier or other liqueur
(Bailey's, Triple Sec, Kahlua)
1 ½ pounds bittersweet chocolate
cocoa and or powdered sugar

Simmer cream in saucepan. When cream comes to a boil, remove from
heat and add chopped chocolate and butter. Stir with wire whish or
wooden spoon until thick and smooth. Pour into bowl and continue to
beat, adding liqueur of choice. Refrigerate until cool and firm – overnight
is best.

When chocolate is firm, shape into one inch balls with scoop or spoon.
Place on a parchment covered baking sheet. Makes approximately 36
truffle centers. Freeze.

Melt 1 1/2 pounds of chocolate in top of double boiler. Pour onto
parchment covered baking sheet. Gently roll truffle centers through
chocolate until coated. Place on clean parchment covered baking sheet.
This layer can also be done with white baking chocolate (make sure
it's the kind that melts – and spoon it on top of your truffles, to avoid
marbling the two chocolates, unless that is your intention).

Dust with cocoa or powdered sugar or grated orange peel. Or not.

(The recipe can be quadrupled; pour into four plastic 1 quart containers,
add different liqueurs or grounds nuts and raisins, or dried cherries or
dates...), then roll in different coatings

Store in airtight container in refrigerator.
For presentation, place Truffles in gold foil candy papers or cups.

1979

California Journal
January, 1979

An African American/Cherokee/Irish doctor named Travis Quinn came to dinner at The Gingerbread Farm last night, all 6'6" of him with skin the color of cocoa and hair the combination you'd imagine from that DNA - a soft, fluffy black afro with red highlights. His contribution to the potluck was Green Sauce and an introduction to Bragg's Liquid Aminos.

Peanut Sauce
Glory

Makes about two cups:

Sauté 2 cloves minced garlic in 1 Tablespoon hot peanut oil.

Place in food processor with:

1/2 to 3/4 cup peanut butter
2 Tablespoons sesame oil
2 chunks ginger, peeled and finely chopped
1 teaspoon sugar
3 Tablespoons Bragg Liquid Aminos* or soy sauce
chili paste, to taste, optional

Set aside.

*un-fermented, organic soy sauce

Veggie Burrito
Glory

Stir-fry, in peanut oil, assorted bite-sized veggies, such as:

Carrots, celery, zucchini, onion, broccoli, peppers, mushrooms

Cook 1 cup Basmati rice in 1 3/4 cups water and a pinch of salt

Just before serving, heat Peanut Sauce through. Do not cook it – it will separate.

Place some rice, some of the veggie mixture and some sauce in a whole wheat or flour tortilla, pour over a little more sauce and serve immediately with **Cilantro Pesto** and/or **Green Sauce**.

Cilantro Pesto
Emma
makes 1 cup

2 cups cilantro, large stems removed
1/2 cup pine nuts
1/4 cup chopped green onion
1/2 teaspoon Serrano chili, chopped and seeded
1 teaspoon salt
1/4 cup olive oil

In a food processor, pulse the cilantro, almonds, onion, chili, and salt until well blended. With the food processor running, slowly add the olive oil.

Whatever you don't use, you can freeze. Line an ice cube tray with plastic wrap and fill in the individual cube spaces with the pesto. Freeze and remove from the ice tray, put in a sealed freezer bag for future use.

Green Sauce
Dr. T

3 avocados, peeled and pitted
3 green tomatoes
4 fresh tomatillos
3 cloves garlic, peeled
2 Jalapeno peppers, seeded and halved, optional
handful of fresh cilantro
1 cup sour cream, optional
salt to taste

Place tomatoes, husked tomatillos, garlic, and jalapenos in a saucepan with enough water to cover. Bring to a boil, and simmer for 15 minutes. Remove from heat, drain, and cool.

Place avocados, the cooked vegetables, sour cream, and cilantro in food processor, and process until smooth. Season to taste with salt. Cover, and refrigerate until ready to serve.

**Houmous, Hummus, Homous, Humus,
Homus, Hommos, Hoummos, Humous**
whichever...
Black E. Brown

2 1/2 cups dried chickpeas
1/2 teaspoon soda

1 teaspoon salt
1 cup lemon juice
1 cup tahini
2 cloves garlic, pressed or chopped
3 Tablespoons olive oil
dash of Bragg's Liquid Aminos
1 teaspoon ground cumin
1/2 cup cilantro or parsley

(reserve some cooked chickpeas)

Soak chickpeas overnight in water and soda. Replace with fresh water
and cook one hour or until tender. Drain. Place in food processor with
lemon juice, tahini, garlic. Process until smooth. Add olive oil and blend.
Add cilantro and blend. Place in serving dish. Garnish with parsley and a
few cooked chickpeas.

Chickpea Biryani
Silver Harper

2 Tablespoons ghee*
or browned butter
2 cloves garlic, minced
1 medium onion, chopped
2 stalks celery, chopped
2 carrots, peeled and chopped
1/4 teaspoon each
cardamom, cloves,
cayenne, ginger,
mace, coriander
1/2 teaspoon cinnamon
1 teaspoon cumin

1 3/4 cup water
1 cup Basmati rice
1 can chickpeas
½ cup raisins

In a heavy-bottomed pot, sauté garlic, onion, celery and carrots in ghee or browned butter. Add spices, water, rice, chickpeas and raisins. Cover and simmer about 25 minutes or bake in a 350° oven for about half an hour. Fluff before serving.

*clarified butter, used in Indian cooking

Maui Onion Rings
Chuck Waggoner

1 1/4 cup flour
1 Tablespoon cornstarch
salt and pepper
1 12-ounce bottle of ale
3 Maui or other sweet onions
vegetable
or peanut oil for deep-frying

Cut onions into 1/4 inch thick slices. Heat oil in deep-fryer to 400°.

Combine flour, cornstarch and salt and pepper in large bowl. Whisk in ale until a smooth batter forms.

Coat onion rings with batter. Gently add to hot oil without crowding and cook until golden brown. Remove with slotted spoon and drain on paper towels. Serve immediately.

California Journal
November, 1979
The Rock House

This never happened in Ohio! There we were, at sunset on a Saturday night, sitting on the deck overlooking the rocks on which Emma's house perches, in the Highlands, toward Big Sur, the shining sea spread out before us like pale blue glass. Not a ripple of water or any boats in sight; except, all at once, Sooz looked up, grabbed the telescope, and yelled, "Oh my God! It's the QE2, really!" And it was indeed our backdrop to this amazing, lovely event.

We watched the QE2 pass slowly by on the calm, majestic Pacific. Bright sunlight bathed us. We sat in comfy deck chairs- Emma, Sooz, Marc, Albert, Dan Hoops and me, cocktails in hand. We were discussing what to have for dinner, planning to use whatever we could find in the house. Emma said, I have a hankering for mollusks.

Dan, who had been dozing in a lounge chair, perked up, and said, OK. Cool. Got butter and stuff?

Sure, of course, said Emma, grinning.

So far, I was clueless - my mid-western roots were showing…

Just you wait, Emma said.

Dan doffed most of his clothes and, armed with a satchel, screwdriver and a personal shaker of Martini, climbed over the deck railing, crawled down over the outcropping of rocks and disappeared for about an hour. We could hear scraping and sloshing water. The occasional "Dang it!"

He was prying our dinner off the rocks! We were getting hungry when it got quiet. Suddenly, Dan reappeared, slipping back over the railing, dripping wet, boxers clinging to his skin, smelling like salt and fish and seaweed, holding a bulging sack, and smiling like a crazy man.

Mussels off the Rocks

2 pounds live mussels
1 Tablespoon unsalted butter
3/4 cup white wine
2 chopped scallions or 1 chopped shallot
2 cloves chopped garlic
salt and pepper to taste
2 cans plum tomatoes
fresh or dried oregano and parsley

With a wiggly motion, pull off "beard," the hairy bit on each mussel that helps the mussel attach to the rock of choice. Heat butter over medium-high heat in a large, wide-bottomed pot with a lid. Sauté the shallot or green onion until it is soft but not browned. Add the garlic cloves if using -- if you are using green garlic, leave it out for now.

At this point, 2 cans of plum tomatoes, parsley and oregano may be added to create a marinara. Leave out for a more traditional steamed mussel dish.

Add the white wine and bring to a boil. Add the mussels in one layer if possible. Cover pot and let mussels steam for 3-8 minutes.

As soon as most of the mussels are open, turn off heat and toss in garlic.

Cover for a minute while you prepare bowls and plates.

Spoon out plenty of mussels and broth. If the mussels aren't salty enough on their own, serve salt. Throw out any unopened mussels.

A Charles Dickens Christmas Invitation
from Emma and Marc Mann

"Heaped up on the floor, to form a kind of throne, were turkeys, geese, game, poultry... mince pies, plum pudding, barrels of oysters, red-hot chestnuts, cherry-cheeked apples, juicy oranges, luscious pears, immense twelfth cakes, and seething bowls of punch, that made the chamber dim with their delicious steam. In easy state upon this couch, there sat a jolly Giant, glorious to see; who bore a glowing torch, in shape not unlike Plenty's horn, and held it up, high up, to shed its light on Scrooge, as he came peeping around the corner.

"Come in!" exclaimed the Ghost. "Come in! and know me better, man!"

A Christmas Carol

Dear Friends,

In America, Christmas wasn't declared a national holiday until 1870, and was against the law in Boston from 1659-1681, the Puritans considering it a pagan event. Oliver Cromwell cancelled Christmas in 1645, to "rid England of its decadence." We thank Charles II, who brought the celebration of Christmas back when the monarchy was restored post-Cromwell, and Queen Victoria especially, for giving Prince Albert a Christmas tree, reviving carols and establishing the roast turkey as the traditional Christmas bird for dinner. Mr. Dickens is given much credit for spreading its popularity in "A Christmas Carol," with its spirit of family, charity, good will toward man, and all that.

We ignite our 1979 holiday spirit
with a celebration a la Charles Dickens
from soup to nuts
including decorations, dress and drinks
We invite you to join us
for this Victorian Christmas
6pm Saturday, December 22
Rock House, The Highlands
Carmel
Emma and Marc Mann
RSVP

A Charles Dickens Christmas Menu

Charles Dickens'
Very Own Christmas Punch
Oysters Ceviche
Chestnut Soup
Turkey Legs
Cornish Pasties*
Toad in the Hole**
Brussels Sprouts
with Leeks and Bacon
Christmas Plum Pudding
Rum Butter or Hard Sauce
Champagne and other Spirits

recipe page 172

**recipe page 175*

Charles Dickens' Very Own Christmas Punch 1847
In his own words

Peel into a very strong common basin (which may be broken, in case of accident, without damage to the owner's peace or pocket) the rinds of three lemons, cut very thin, and with as little as possible of the white coating between the peel and the fruit, attached.

Add a double-handfull of lump sugar (good measure), a pint of good old rum, and a large wineglass full of brandy — if it not be a large claret-glass, say two. Set this on fire, by filling a warm silver spoon with the spirit, lighting the contents at a wax taper, and pouring them gently in. Let it burn for three or four minutes at least, stirring it from time to time. Then extinguish it by covering the basin with a tray, which will immediately put out the flame. Then squeeze in the juice of the three lemons, and add a quart of boiling water.

Stir the whole well, cover it up for five minutes, and stir again. At this crisis (having skimmed off the lemon pips with a spoon) you may taste. If not sweet enough, add sugar to your liking, but observe that it will be a little sweeter presently.

Pour the whole into a jug, tie a leather or coarse cloth over the top, so as to exclude the air completely, and stand it in a hot oven ten minutes, or on a hot stove one quarter of an hour. Keep it until it comes to table in a warm place near the fire, but not too hot. If it be intended to stand three or four hours, take half the lemon-peel out, or it will acquire a bitter taste. The same punch allowed to cool by degrees, and then iced, is delicious. It requires less sugar when made for this purpose. If you wish to produce it bright, strain it into bottles through silk. These proportions and directions will, of course, apply to any quantity.**

**A Christmas Carol   **From a letter to a friend*

Oh! But he was a tight-fisted hand at the grindstone, Scrooge!
A squeezing, wrenching, grasping, scraping, clutching, covetous old sinner! Hard
and sharp as flint, from which no steel had ever struck out generous fire: secret, self-
*contained, and solitary as an oyster."**

Oysters Ceviche

12 fresh, raw oysters
1 medium onion
1 tomato
1 cup fresh corn,
roasted and caramelized
in 1 Tablespoon butter
(frozen corn can be used
if thawed
and drained
before roasting)

juice of 1 lime
1 Jalapeño pepper
1 Tablespoon chopped parsley
1 Tablespoon chopped cilantro
salt and pepper to taste

Dice onion and tomato and mix together with the corn. Chop the Jalapeño, removing seeds and add to mixture. Add parsley, cilantro, and lime juice and mix all ingredients well.

Shuck the oysters and place the raw oysters back on half a shell each. Place a generous spoonful of the ceviche mixture onto each Oyster. Or, Oysters can be broiled for five minutes before adding ceviche mixture.

**A Christmas Carol*

Chestnut Bisque

2 Tablespoons unsalted butter, for sauté
1 medium onion, chopped
1 stalk celery, chopped
1 carrot, chopped
1 clove garlic, chopped
kosher salt
4 cups chicken stock
1 bay leaf
1 pound roasted chestnuts

1/2 cup heavy cream
1 Tablespoon sherry

3 Tablespoons unsalted butter for crostini
2 cups thinly sliced baguette
vegetable oil
4 cups Italian parsley, washed and dried
1 teaspoon cornstarch
salt

A Christmas Carol

Melt the butter in soup-pot over medium heat. Add the onion, celery, carrot, garlic and 1/2 teaspoon salt; cook, stirring, about 8 minutes, or until softened. Add chicken stock and bay leaf. Simmer 5 minutes. Chop chestnuts and add to pan. Simmer until chestnuts and vegetables are tender, about 10 minutes. Remove bay leaf. Using a hand-help soup blender, puree the soup until smooth. Strain through a sieve into another saucepan and bring to a simmer over medium-high heat. Add the cream, sherry, and salt to taste. Keep warm.

For the crostini, melt the butter in skillet over medium heat. Add the baguette slices and cook, turning once, and stirring until golden, about 3 minutes. Ladle the soup into bowls and top with the crostini and fried parsley.

Turkey Legs

1 cup salt
1 cup white sugar
8 turkey drumsticks
4 cups white wine
1 cup brown sugar
1/2 cup molasses
1/4 cup Balsamic vinegar
1 cup ketchup
4 Tablespoons Worcestershire sauce
3 Tablespoons dried sage
3 Tablespoons dried thyme

Pour enough water into a large pot to cover the turkey legs and dissolve the salt and white sugar. Immerse the turkey legs in the brine, cover and refrigerate for at least 2 hours.

Preheat oven to 325°. In a saucepan, stir together the white wine, brown sugar, molasses, vinegar, ketchup and Worcestershire sauce. Bring to a boil, and cook until reduced by half. Season with half the herbs. Add salt and pepper to taste.

Remove the turkey legs from the brine, rinse off salt and sugar and pat dry with paper towels. Discard the brine. Heat a large oven-proof skillet over medium-high heat. Fry the turkey legs, turning often, until browned on all sides. Place the pan with the turkey into the oven.

Roast 45 minutes, uncovered. Remove and turn legs over. Season with remaining thyme and sage, and baste legs with sauce. Return to oven for an additional 45 minutes, basting often, until legs are tender. Serve with basting sauce.

8 cups Brussels sprouts
1/2 cup water
4 bacon strips, chopped
salt and pepper
1 large leek
2 Tablespoons olive oil
1 clove garlic, crushed
1 Tablespoon cider vinegar
1/2 cup fresh parsley, chopped

Trim ends from Brussels sprouts and cut each sprout in half. In large skillet, place Brussels sprouts and water; cover and cook on medium until tender – about 10 minutes. Drain. Transfer to large bowl and set aside.

Add bacon to skillet and cook on medium 5 to 6 minutes or until browned, stirring occasionally. With slotted spoon, transfer bacon to paper towels to drain. Keep skillet on heat.

Add sprouts, 1/4 teaspoon salt, and 1/4 teaspoon black pepper to skillet. Cook on medium-high 6 to 8 minutes or until Brussels sprouts are browned, stirring frequently. Remove from pan; keep warm.

Clean and drain leek. Add olive oil to same skillet and heat. Add leek, garlic, 1/4 teaspoon salt, and 1/4 teaspoon black pepper; cook until leek is tender and browned, stirring frequently. Add bacon, Brussels sprouts, and cider vinegar; cook 2 minutes, stirring occasionally. To serve, stir parsley into vegetables in skillet; transfer to serving bowl.

Christmas Plum Pudding

1 cup currants
1 cup golden raisins
1 1/2 cup raisins
1 cup flour
2 cups stale breadcrumbs
1 cup shredded suet
1 cup dark brown sugar
1/4 cup chopped almonds
4   beaten eggs
2 Tablespoon Guinness
juice of 1 lemon
juice of 1 orange
1/2 Tablespoon allspice
1 Tablespoon nutmeg
1/2 cup rum
2 Tablespoons candied fruit peel

Mix all ingredients together in a large bowl and put in one 7-8 cup
English pudding bowl or 2 smaller bowls. Leave at least 1 inch at the top
of bowl so that the pudding has room to expand. Cover with two sheets
of waxed paper and a layer of aluminum foil. Tie the top tightly around
the rim of the basin with string and make a handle so that the pudding
can be lifted. Lower the pudding bowl into a large pan of boiling water
with a saucer upturned on the bottom. The water should come up the
sides of the pudding bowl about 3/4. Cover and simmer for at least 7
hours. Check that the water does not drop below 3/4 of the way up. Add
hot more water if necessary.

Remove the pudding and store in a cool place. When planning to serve,
boil pudding for two hours in the same way. Remove the cover and turn
the pudding over onto a serving platter. Just before serving, warm a little
brandy or rum in a saucepan pour it over the pudding, and light with a
match.

Serve with Rum Butter or Hard Sauce.

**A Christmas Carol*

Rum Butter

1 pound brown sugar
1/2 pound butter
1 cup rum
1/4 teaspoon grated nutmeg

Melt butter. Do not let boil. Beat in sugar. Stir in rum, a tablespoon at a time and then the nutmeg. Place mixture into a serving bowl and use when set.

Sealed in an airtight container, Rum Butter will keep for over a month in refrigerator, but DO refrigerate, as the sugar will re-crystalize.

Hard Sauce

1 cup powdered sugar
1/3 cup butter
2 teaspoons rum (or vanilla)
Using the back of a wooden spoon, cream sugar into butter. Add rum (or vanilla).

Refrigerate until firm. Serve over hot plum pudding.

A Christmas Carol

1980

California Journal
New Year's Morning
1980

Ah. And 1979 rolls into 1980 and rolls me forward into the unknown. This relationship wobbles, big time. Can this marriage be saved? Only the *Ladies Home Journal* knows for sure. My guess is no, but then, who am I to cast a vote? I am in the middle of this, with no objectivity whatsoever.

We go to parties, we put on happy faces, we drink too much champagne, we go home silent and in shadow. The food is good, but who cares? We are too sad to eat it. With Billy off at boarding school, our marital glue is dissolving.

'Shrooms and Shrimp

20 large white mushrooms, stems removed
1 cup baby shrimp, raw
2 Tablespoons butter
1 clove garlic, finely diced
1 dash hot sauce
1 cup breadcrumbs
3/4 cup grated Romano cheese

Lightly grease a 9x13 inch baking dish.

Sauté baby shrimp in hot butter and garlic. Set aside and chop when cooled. Combine with remaining ingredients. Spoon about 2 teaspoons of shrimp mixture into the cap of each mushroom and place, stuffing side up, in prepared baking dish. Sprinkle more Romano cheese on top. Cover and refrigerate for at least 3 hours or overnight to blend the flavors and firm up the stuffing.

Preheat an oven to 400°. Uncover baking dish and bake mushrooms for about 15 minutes, until the cheese is browned and bubbling.

1 pound pitted dates
1/2 pound bacon sliced into quarters

Place bacon on baking sheet covered with parchment. Bake at 325° for about 5 minutes, until partially cooked, but not browned.

Wrap each date with a strip of bacon and secure with a wooden toothpick. Broil on low 3 minutes, turn dates, and continue broiling 3 to 4 minutes longer, or until browned.

Drain on paper towel and serve warm.

1 medium onion, chopped
1 garlic clove, chopped
2 medium ham hocks
2 cups dried black eyes peas, picked through to discard pits, rocks, etc.
2 Tablespoons olive oil
3 cups water
1/2 pound collard greens
1 teaspoon cider vinegar

In a soup pot, cook onion and garlic in oil over moderate heat, stirring occasionally, until onion is golden. Add ham hocks, water and black-eyed peas and cook according to directions on bag until almost done.

While this is cooking, discard stems and center ribs from collards and finely chop leaves. Add collards and simmer until collards are tender, about 20 minutes.

Season soup with salt and pepper and stir in vinegar.

**Flossie's
Award Winning Blue Cornbread**

1 pound loaf pan
baking spray

1 1/2 cups organic white flour
1/2 cup blue cornmeal
1/4 cup brown sugar
2 teaspoons baking powder
1 teaspoon baking soda
1 teaspoon salt
2 eggs
1 cup buttermilk
1/4 cup melted butter

Options:
1 large green onion, chopped
1/2 bunch cilantro, chopped

Preheat oven to 350°. Coat pan with vegetable spray.
Mix flour, cornmeal, sugar, baking powder, baking soda and salt in large bowl. In another bowl, beat together eggs, buttermilk and butter. Mix gently with dry ingredients, folding in ingredients carefully. Place in prepared pan. Bake for about 45 minutes, or until inserted skewer or knife comes out clean. Turn out onto cooling rack and cool slightly before cutting.

1 large onion, thinly sliced
2 Tablespoons unsalted butter
4 pounds sauerkraut, rinsed and drained
2 Gala, Fuji, or Red Delicious apples, thinly sliced
1 cup dry white wine
1 to 2 tablespoons packed dark brown sugar

Cook onion in butter in a large, heavy pot over medium-high heat until golden, about 6 minutes, stirring occasionally. Add sauerkraut, apples, and wine and bring to a simmer.

Cover pot, reduce heat and simmer until sauerkraut is very tender, about 2 hours. Before serving, add 1-2 tablespoons brown sugar, salt and pepper to taste.

Moneybags Kale
*The green leaves look like money –
symbolic for prosperity in the New Year*

3 bunches kale,
stems removed,
washed and chopped,
1 onion, chopped
1 clove garlic, minced
2 Tablespoons butter
1 Tablespoons olive oil
6 Tablespoons Balsamic vinegar
4-6 Tablespoons brown sugar
squeeze of lemon juice and
or lemon zest
salt and pepper to taste

Sauté onion and garlic in hot butter/oil mixture. Add chopped kale
and a little water and cover. Simmer on low heat, adding more water if
necessary, for about 30 minutes, or until kale is tender. Remove cover,
add Balsamic vinegar and brown sugar and simmer for about five
minutes, or until the liquid is mostly absorbed. Serve warm or cold as a
salad.

Lemon or Orange Pound Bundt Cake
A ring, symbol of eternity, brings good luck

3 1/3 cups sugar
10 eggs
1 pound butter, softened
zest of two lemons (or oranges)
3 Tablespoons lemon or orange juice
1 Tablespoon vanilla
4 cups sifted flour

Place sugar and eggs in a Kitchen Aid or mixer. Set on medium and mix for ten minutes, until soft ribbons form and it turns pale yellow. Add softened butter and blend well. Slowly add flour, 1/3 at a time, until blended in. Add remaining ingredients and blend until smooth. Pour into well-sprayed Bundt pan and bake covered with foil for 30 minutes. Uncover and continue baking for 1 1/4 hours. Cool.

*Glory's Birth Year
The Year of The Pig 1947*

The Pig is a fun and energetic being, filled with patience and understanding. People born under the sign of the Pig enjoy life and all it has to offer, including family, friends and food. Pigs are honest and thoughtful and expect the same of other people. Pigs will do just about anything for a friend in need.

*Chinese New Year 1980
The Year of the Monkey*

Monkeys are geniuses, gregarious, intelligent, curious and clever. Nothing is too hard for Monkeys and they catch on quickly. Monkeys are inventive, love challenges and have a deep respect and understanding of knowledge.

Monkeys like being in the limelight.

*Glory Sugar Baker Parker,
born in the Year of the Pig,
destined for change
in the year of the Monkey*

Chinese New Year Menu

Jiaozi Dumplings
For Prosperity

Dipping Sauce

Longevity Noodles
*Symbolizing a long life –
but only if they are not cut!*

Buddha's Delight

Fortune Cookies

Jiaozi Dumplings
For Prosperity

Jiaozi dough:
3 cups all-purpose flour
Up to 1 1/4 cups cold water
1/4 teaspoon salt

Filling:
1 cup ground pork or beef
1 Tablespoon soy sauce
1 teaspoon salt
1 Tablespoon Chinese rice wine or dry sherry
1/4 teaspoon freshly ground white pepper, or to taste
3 Tablespoons sesame oil
1/2 green onion, finely minced
1 1/2 cups finely shredded Napa cabbage
4 Tablespoons shredded bamboo shoots
2 slices fresh ginger, finely minced
1 clove garlic, peeled and finely minced

Stir the salt into the flour. Slowly stir in the cold water, adding as much as is necessary to form a smooth dough. Don't add more water than is necessary. Knead the dough into a smooth ball. Cover the dough and let it rest for at least 30 minutes.

While the dough is resting, prepare the filling ingredients. Add the soy sauce, salt, rice wine and white pepper to the meat, stirring in only one direction. Add the remaining ingredients, stirring in the same direction, and mix well.

To make the dumpling dough: knead the dough until it forms a smooth ball. Divide the dough into 60 pieces. Roll each piece out into a circle about 3-inches in diameter.

Place a small portion (about 1 level tablespoon) of the filling into the middle of each wrapper. Wet the edges of the dumpling with water. Fold the dough over the filling into a half moon shape and pinch the edges to seal. Continue with the remainder of the dumplings.

To cook, bring a large pot of water to a boil. Add half the dumplings, giving them a gentle stir so they don't stick together. Bring the water to a boil a second time, and add 1/2 cup of cold water. Cover and repeat, bringing water to a boil again. When the dumplings come to a boil for a third time, they are ready. Drain and remove. If desired, they can be pan-fried at this point.

Dipping Sauce

1/2 cup light soy sauce
1/4 cup red wine vinegar
2 teaspoons minced ginger
2 Tablespoons brown sugar
2 spring onions (green onions, scallions), chopped

In a small bowl, combine the soy sauce, red wine vinegar and minced ginger. Set aside.

In a small heavy saucepan, melt the brown sugar on high heat, stirring rapidly, until it is just melted but not burnt. Add the soy sauce and red wine mixture. Bring to boil until brown sugar is melted again (it will harden temporarily after the soy sauce mixture is added).

Remove from the heat, pour into a serving dish and garnish with the chopped spring onions.

Longevity Noodles
Symbolizing a long life – but only if they are not cut!

8 cups water
1 teaspoon salt
1/2 pound dried thin egg noodles or spaghetti

3 cups chicken broth or stock
1 Tablespoon soy sauce, or to taste
1 teaspoon sesame oil
2 teaspoons cornstarch mixed with 4 teaspoons water
White or black pepper, to taste

2 eggs, lightly beaten
3 green onions (spring onions), finely chopped
1/2 - 2/3 cup chopped cooked meat or poultry

Bring the salted water to a boil and parboil the noodles, using chopsticks to separate them. Rinse the noodles repeatedly in cold water and drain thoroughly. Divide the noodles equally among soup bowls.

Bring the broth or stock to a boil over medium heat. Stir in the soy sauce, sesame oil, and pepper. Give the cornstarch and water a quick re-stir and stir it in. Remove the saucepan from the heat. Add the beaten egg, pouring it slowly through the tines of a fork and stirring rapidly in one direction for about 1 minute.

Pour the hot broth over the noodles. Garnish with the chopped meat, green onion and cooked greens.

Buddha's Delight

It is a Buddhist tradition that no animal or fish should be killed on the first day of the lunar year. Vegetables are considered to be purifying, and many of the ingredients in this dish, from lily buds to fungus, have significance.

4 dried Shiitake or Chinese black mushrooms
1/2 cup dried lily buds
4 dried bean curd sticks
8 ounces bamboo shoots
6 fresh water chestnuts
2 large carrots
1 cup shredded Napa cabbage
4 ounces snow peas
1/4 cup canned gingko nuts
1 piece of ginger, crushed

Sauce:
Dark Veggie Stock*
1 Tablespoon Chinese rice wine or dry sherry
1 Tablespoon dark soy sauce
1 teaspoon sugar
1/2 teaspoon sesame oil

vegetable or peanut oil for stir-frying, as needed

In separate bowls, soak the mushrooms, dried lily buds, and dried bean curd sticks in hot water for 20 to 30 minutes to soften. Squeeze out any excess liquid. Reserve the mushroom soaking liquid, straining it if necessary to remove any grit. Remove the stems and cut the mushroom tops in half if desired.

Slice the bamboo shoots. Peel and finely chop the water chestnuts. Peel the carrots, cut in half, and cut lengthwise into thin strips. Shred the Napa cabbage. String the snow peas and cut in half. Drain the gingko nuts. Crush the ginger.

Combine the reserved mushroom soaking liquid or vegetarian stock with the Chinese rice wine or sherry, dark soy sauce, sugar and sesame oil. Set aside.

Honey Baby Darlin' Book One – The Farm, page 102

Heat the wok over medium-high to high heat. Add 2 tablespoons oil to the heated wok.

When the oil is hot, add the carrots. Stir-fry for 1 minute, and add the dried mushrooms and lily buds. Stir-fry for 1 minute, and add the water chestnuts, bamboo shoots, snow peas and ginger. Stir in the shredded cabbage and gingko nuts. Add the bean curd sticks.

Add the sauce ingredients and bring to a boil. Cover, turn down the heat and let the vegetables simmer for 5 minutes. Taste and add salt or other seasonings as desired. Serve hot.

Fortune Cookies

Fortune cookies are like little tiny crepes on a baking sheet - spread out evenly, gently tilting the baking sheet back and forth as needed. Wearing cotton gloves makes it easier to handle and shape the hot cookies. This recipe makes about 10 cookies.

2 large egg whites
1/2 teaspoon pure vanilla extract
1/2 teaspoon pure almond extract
3 Tablespoons vegetable oil
8 Tablespoons all-purpose flour
1 1/2 teaspoons cornstarch
1/4 teaspoon salt
8 Tablespoons granulated sugar
3 teaspoons water

Write fortunes on pieces of paper that are 3 1/2 inches long and 1/2 inch wide. Preheat oven to 300°. Line 2 baking sheets with parchment.

In a medium bowl, lightly beat the egg white, vanilla extract, almond extract and vegetable oil until frothy, but not stiff.

Sift the flour, cornstarch, salt and sugar into a separate bowl. Stir the water into the flour mixture.

Add the flour into the egg white mixture and stir until you have a smooth batter. The batter should not be runny, but should drop easily off a wooden spoon.

Place level tablespoons of batter onto the cookie sheet, spacing them at least 3 inches apart. Gently tilt the baking sheet back and forth and from side to side so that each tablespoon of batter forms into a circle 4 inches in diameter.

Bake until the outer 1/2-inch of each cookie turns golden brown and they are easy to remove from the baking sheet with a spatula (14 - 15 minutes).

Working quickly, remove the cookie with a spatula and flip it over in your hand. Place a fortune in the middle of a cookie. To form the fortune cookie shape, fold the cookie in half and gently pull the edges downward over the rim of a glass or wooden spoon. Place the finished cookie in the cup of a muffin tin so that it keeps its shape. Continue with the rest of the cookies.

會發現在新的一年幸福

You will find happiness
in the New Year

And, so, we come to the
END
of
The Gingerbread Farm,
the second Farm in the
Honey Baby Darlin' series

Stay tuned for **Golden Gate Retreat Farm,** the third farm in the series, as Glory steps into life on the road, alone, as a professional cook, and begins to rattle her pots and pans for gurus, spas, movie stars, and artists.

www.honeybabydarlin.com

Acknowledgments

I thank all my relations and friends, particularly:

My cousin, Babe, for being one of my biggest fans, always;

Joan Marsh, editor most dedicated;

Charles Gruwell, for titles with meaning;

Chef Joe;

Gail Lindus, for friendship, assistance and editing/proofing skills;

Bill Fairweather, for providing friendship and an on-book-tour-home-away-from-home in Bath;

All the real people who have salted and peppered these pages with memories;

My brothers, Mark and Jess, who cheer me on;

My son, Michael, who calls me the "miracle mom" – I just love that;

Rev. Joan Gattuso, lifelong friend;

Lucky Valley Press;

Nan, who reminded me of the ending;

David, who is my greatest gift;

And Squeaks and Smooch, who provide warm fur into which I can press my nose and amusing kitty entertainment, as long as I provide a lap and dinner.

Ginna BB Gordon
Carmel 2012

Honey Baby Darlin' Book One – The Farm
Glory's mind is opened to food, cooking and sustenance, watching her
mother and others at the Farm create magic and love.

The Gingerbread Farm
Glory matures into young womanhood, stirs a dash of trouble into the
simmering soup of her life and sets off for Carmel, California, where she
plants a garden, rears her child and considers the thoughts and nutritional
habits of a few select spiritual teachers and good cooks. It is the 70s, and her
pantry bulges with whole grains, the windowsills carry trays of sprouting
seeds, and chickens once again scratch 'n scrabble in the backyard.

Golden Gate Retreat Farm - to the stars
Glory cooks for gurus, spas, rock stars, and other illustrious beings while
managing her own affairs. She lives in a 400 square foot tipi at a retreat farm
and discovers an enlightening genealogical fact. As she travels the west coast
in her red Jeep Cherokee, Glory creates kitchen temples of nourishment
while serving up sustenance in warm bowls. She writes a cookbook about
Ayurveda, the eastern lifestyle set forth by ancient rishis while sitting in
meditation on rocks in the Himalayas. She becomes a grandmother.

Lucky Valley Farm - my Carmel
Glory, longing for a home and a hearth of her own, settles back to Carmel, a
Café and, eventually, finally, finds herself in the arms of her sweetie. Then she
writes another book. And then another.

Ginna has cooked for movie stars, Tibetan Lamas, gurus, and teachers; for retreat and conference centers; and for her own catering companies and cafes, in very unusual situations (cook tents, tall ships, mountain lodges, trailers on a movie set, spa kitchens, campfires).

Ginna was founding executive chef at Deepak Chopra's Center for Well Being in La Jolla, California, where she designed the original kitchen, created the spa guest meals and operated a 24-seat café at the Center.

Ginna and David Simon, MD (who passed away in 2012), the Chopra Center medical director, co-authored ***A Simple Celebration: a vegetarian cookbook for body mind and spirit,*** (Ginna Bell Bragg/David Simon, MD, Harmony Books/Random House, 1997, ISBN0-517-70732-2). This book is for the vegetarian home cook interested in the practice of Ayurveda, the lifestyle based on ancient East Indian rishi-knowledge. Using Western ingredients, Ginna offers meals and a reference guide for ingredients and body types.

Ginna's 2011 release, ***Honey, Baby, Darlin', Book One - The Farm,*** is the first part of *a serial memoir about cooking, love and the love of cooking.*

Part Two of the series, **The Gingerbread Farm**, grows Glory into a real cook. **Golden Gate Retreat Farm - to the stars** takes her out into the world and her cooking career, and **Lucky Valley Farm - my Carmel** brings her home again.

Ginna lives with her husband, singer/web design guru, David Gordon, and their cats, Squeaks and Smooch, in Carmel, California.